DARK CONJURINGS

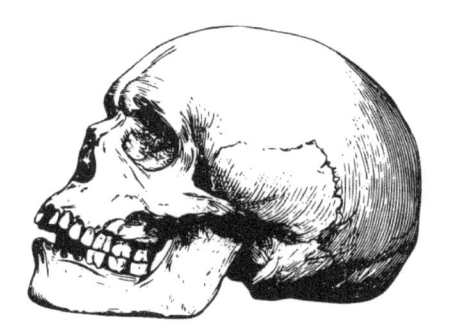

A Short Fiction Horror Anthology

E
EagleHeightsPress

Dark Conjurings: *Short Fiction Horror Anthology*
© 2019 Eagle Heights Press

This is a work of fiction. All characters, events, or organizations in it are products of the authors' imaginations or used fictitiously. All rights reserved. No part of this publication may be reproduced, stored in a retrieval system or transmitted in any form or by any means, electronic, mechanical, photocopying, recording or otherwise without the prior permission of the publisher or in accordance with the provisions of the Copyright, Designs and Patents Act 1988 or under the terms of any license permitting limited copying issued by the Copyright Licensing Agency. Please purchase only authorized electronic editions, and do not participate in or encourage electronic piracy of copyrighted materials. Thank you for your support of the author's rights.

Foreword ©2019 by Sarah Read
All That Glitters Must Die ©2019 by Jai Lefay
The Shadows Breathe ©2019 by A.R. Reinhardt
Night of the Beast ©2019 by Cassy Crownover
The Doctor and The Lady ©2019 by Delia Remington
The Lady In White ©2019 by Karolyne Cronin
Mystick Tea ©2019 by Mimi Schweid

Eagle Heights Press
414 N. Church St.
Fayette, MO 65248
eagleheightspress.com

Edited by Delia Remington
Cover and Interior Images ©2019 Cassy Crownover
Cover Design by Cassy Crownover and Delia Remington
Interior design by Delia Remington

First Edition: October 2019

Published by: Eagle Heights Press, a division of Eagle Heights L.L.C.

The publisher is not responsible for websites (or their content) that are not owned by the publisher.

Hard Cover (Library Edition): 978-1-947181-15-1
Paperback ISBN-13: 978-1-947181-14-4

Table of Contents

Foreword by Sarah Read 7

All That Glitters Must Die by Jai Lefay 13

The Shadows Breathe by A.R. Reinhardt 57

Night of the Beast by Cassy Crownover 75

The Doctor and The Lady by Delia Remington 91

The Lady In White by Karolyne Cronin 121

Mystick Tea by Mimi Schweid 163

Foreword

By Sarah Reed

ACE of PENTACLES

Foreword

One of the best things about new voices in literature is that they have not been restrained by arbitrary rules or modes of style that paint a homogeneous veil over the more prominent works in a genre. Emerging voices bring fresh tones, new perspectives, and a clear sense that the writer is writing for the sheer joy of storytelling.

Sheer joy might not be the right phrase for these dark tales. Thrill is probably more appropriate, though I believe these six forthcoming authors will take great joy in thrilling you.

Here we have a story about a vampire that's not about the vampire but about the friendships formed among his prey.

A powerful, trapped spirit orchestrates the vengeful haunting of a killer and frees the soul of one of his victims.

A Civil War soldier's camp faces a legendary beast in a dark forest that takes the terror of war to a new level.

A witch faces death itself to save her sister, drawing strength from the love of her life and her family's legacy of power.

We get a glimpse into the tragic truth behind an urban legend and how they become a part of our culture and collective unconscious.

We witness Mary Shelley's grim discovery and subsequent inspiration for the genre that would come to unite us all in these dark conjurings.

You'll get your daily dose of gore, of haunting, of twisted imaginings and familiar tales told from new angles. These six stories draw together classic elements of the horror genre—witches, vampires, ghosts, werewolves, the reanimated dead—and show that tropes are tools that can be used to build a bigger, more diverse genre.

The horror genre was invented by women and other marginalized voices, yet it has a history of excluding us. I, a woman who writes horror, have been told women don't write horror. I've been told my work isn't "really" horror. I've been told by editors whose anthologies contain fewer than 10% women and often zero nonbinary or culturally diverse authors, that they're "just publishing the best stories" as if the problem lies in their inbox and not their worldview. The excuse has grown stale. There are well-established voices in horror everywhere, and in anthologies like this one, we get to see the emergence of a new generation of dark fiction writers.

Horror is in a golden age, perhaps because we need it so much right now. When the scariest books on the bookshelf are in the current affairs section, ghosts are a refuge. A way to work the dread out of our system and train our minds on how to process things like fear, loss, grief, and the looming threat of our planet's mortality.

Take a break from the monsters in the news and face these vampires for a moment. Flex your muscles against the weight of this twitching corpse, so you'll be stronger when the call comes to face the real monsters. They've dialed all but the last number, finger hovering. Are you ready? Read horror, and prepare yourself.

Sarah Read
Appleton, Wisconsin.
September 2019

Sarah Read

Sarah Read is a dark fiction writer in the frozen north of Wisconsin. Her short stories can be found in various journals and anthologies including *The Best Horror of the Year vol 10*. Her novel *The Bone Weaver's Orchard* is now out from Trepidatio Publishing, and her debut collection *Out of Water* will follow in November 2019. She is the Editor-in-Chief of *Pantheon Magazine* and of their associated anthologies, including *Gorgon: Stories of Emergence*. She is an active member of the Horror Writers Association. When she's not staring into the abyss, she knits.

Follow her on Twitter or Instagram @Inkwellmonster, her website www.inkwellmonster.wordpress.com, or on Patreon at https://www.patreon.com/SarahRead.

All That Glitters Must Die

By Jai Lefay

The seventh tarot card was flipped from the pile and placed gently down, only for the table to lurch suddenly beneath it.

"Death? Oh my goodness, I am going to die!"

"Death virtually never means actual death, Audrey, relax, I hmmm..." Lady Lotte of the Mysteries, aka Lotte de Vries, let the cards speak to her and her smile vanished. She looked back up at Audrey and tried to push a fake one into place. Lotte was not meant to let these readings get serious. She was a performer at Ziggy Rose – House of Burlesco, and reading the cards was another part of her act. It was just entertainment to titillate their rich and usually tight-laced clients. She was not meant to do real readings, even for the other girls.

"What do you mean, hmmm? Lotte, am I dying?" Audrey sounded panicked, and the table was still shuddering as she gripped the edge of it for dear life.

Lotte tried to force her lips wider in a smile and make her tone teasing. "Audrey, darling, I am playing with you.

The death card means that part of your life will die. A part that you no longer need."

Lotte was lying. While she might read the cards for entertainment, that did not mean she lacked the true gift to read them. The cards were unfortunately very clear in their message. A violent death was to be expected and soon.

"Oh, you mean like the part of my life that sees me unwed?" Audrey asked, her eyes lighting up at the thought of finally becoming a married woman. She was constantly looking for love and hoping for an engagement but while it had happened for many girls who had then moved on from Ziggy Rose, poor Audrey had not caught anyone's eye in months. A situation that might grow worse if the country did enter the war and begin to send the men overseas.

"Oh yes," Lotte quickly replied, still fake smiling as she reached over the table to gently pat Audrey's hand as it gripped the edge of the small round table. "I know you have been wanting that for so long."

"So very much."

Lotte moved her hand back, fingertips brushing the soft red velvet tablecloth as she flicked each turned card back towards her. She turned them over and placed her hands atop them, removing them from Audrey's sight. "Now, scoot your skirts, you have only twenty minutes before the doors open, and you've smudged your make-up."

Audrey gave Lotte an absent-minded smile as she got up from the table, Lotte assumed she was already lost in thoughts of all the men she hoped might come to woo her. Lotte waited until her friend had moved out of her line of sight before turning the cards back over and completing the reading. There was no mistaking it, Audrey was in very real danger, and while there was a man involved, it was not the kind of "Until death do us part" connection that Audrey was looking for. A man came to end her life, in a most gruesome manner. Lotte feared she knew who he might be.

Astoria had been the latest place to be visited by the Vampire of the Opera as the press had affectionately called this serial killer. Sixteen showgirls in separate cities had been killed in the last six months, four in New York in the last two. The papers reported that the man had fantasies of vampirism, making it appear as if the women had been bitten on the neck before being drained of blood.

Lotte believed it might actually be a vampire, not simply a staging of the victims. Her family had once had dealings with a vampire, and she believed their stories to be true. Law enforcement would not be so easy to convince of that, nor were they likely to believe that Audrey was in danger if Lotte was to go to them. Her seeing death in the cards was not hard evidence for them to act on. No, Lotte could not go to them, which meant that Audrey's only protection was Lotte. Lotte was more than willing to put her own life in danger if she could keep sweet Audrey safe from harm. It was what friends did. But first they needed to get through their responsibilities for the evening, plus

Jack was coming tonight which made Lotte's stomach flutter nervously. He was so handsome, and he liked her.

The dim electric light above her flickered and drew her out of her thoughts. Lotte might have taken that as a bad omen, but it simply always did that. She waited until the bulb stopped flickering and got up. She needed to make certain she was presentable for Jack's arrival.

**

Jack topped up the girls' glasses. His eyes lingered on Lotte as the other young women giggled at his jesting. Lotte smiled but wasn't sure she understood why it was funny. She shrugged that off, enjoying the way that he looked at her across the table. There would be fewer giggles from some of the women if they knew that Jack had been calling on Lotte for the last week. Or if they knew that on Friday night after she finished work, he was actually going to take her out for dinner at a fancy restaurant.

Lotte found it hard to fathom that the son of one of the rich and famous families who holidayed in their mansions in Astoria would be interested in her. Even an illegitimate son. Yet, he truly seemed interested in her, given he made conversation with her and sought to know her, rather than attempting a lazy seduction as many of the rich men did with the pretty staff at Ziggy Rose. Some men did not even do that. And there were more than a few girls who had been hurt beyond repair by their actions, with meagre payments as their only justice.

The thought gave Lotte pause. She looked around from her seat over at the rest of the tables and the bar area. Perhaps she was being fanciful to think that a deranged killer from the papers was Audrey's threat. It could certainly be someone far closer to home. Lotte would be sure to keep an eye on their regulars and any new arrivals who took more than a normal interest in Audrey during or after the show.

"Lotte?"

Lotte startled at the sound of her name and a gentle touch on her wrist. She turned back to the table and caught a look of the evils from Fleur as Jack touched her to try to get her attention. "Are you well, Lady Lotte? You look lost and quite pale."

Lotte forced her second smile of the evening, not wanting to worry the young Astor with her thoughts; nor drive him away with them. "Just fretting I left part of my costume back at the apartment."

Lotte shared a small apartment with Audrey and their friend Sonja. Sonja's parents, the Janssens, owned and ran Ziggy Rose, as well as the apartment. Lotte's roommates were the only two who knew of Jack's interest in Lotte, and both had kept quiet about it at her request. He was, after all, one of the most eligible bachelors who came to the show at the moment, and Lotte did not want anything to ruin her chance with him.

Hence her white lie now. While he had never said anything negative about Lotte reading the cards, that did not mean he would believe her if she told him why she was truly worried right now.

"If you would excuse me," Lotte continued, "I really should double check backstage before we begin the third act. In fact, we should all be getting ready."

She gave Fleur a pointed look, not very keen on leaving the woman alone with Jack. One could only imagine what wiles she might use on him, or the lies she might say about Lotte to try and discredit her. They also should get ready.

The first part of the show with the comedy acts was nearly finishing up, which meant the strong men would be up next and then the girls would take the stage. She gave Jack a small smile. "I will see you after the show?"

"I will be here waiting," Jack replied, smiling at Lotte who managed a bright, genuine smile this time before she left with the other women.

**

Audrey and Fleur were on first with their contortion act. Lotte did not usually watch their acts. The way they fit into those small trunks made her feel funny inside. Normally she stayed in the dressing room, but tonight she needed to keep an eye out for Audrey. She lingered instead by the stage door, a heavy black curtain that had replaced the squeaky wooden door about a year ago, the same time that Lotte had become a named act in the show. From this spot looking through a small gap between the curtain and door frame, she could watch most of the club.

It was mostly gentlemen in the audience now. Only a few had brought their wives or mistresses along for the evening. The men were enjoying the display, while many of the women looked horrified watching the acts of contortion. One man watching stuck out to Lotte. He was not dressed the same as many of the other men in their impeccably tailored suits. His suit seemed old and perhaps not even his. The sleeves did not reach down to his wrists. He was large and clearly muscular beneath the suit, and his skin was more tanned than that of the others. It was a status symbol to be pale, a sign that you did no labour. Lotte could have been very elite. She was always pale, the sun only ever turning her bright red and never brown.

The man seemed to be enjoying watching Fleur and Audrey, but that was no different than anyone else. So, she let the curtain drop back into place and returned to the side of the stage. She grabbed her scarves that hung from the top of her skirts, adjusted the ties at the far edge of each to slide them over her fingers, and flapped her arms, feeling like a brightly coloured bird. She took her mark and waited for her own entrance. For all she was pale, there was something exotic about her look thanks to her paternal grandmother's line. Because of that, she played the parts of tarot reader and dancing gypsy in the show.

Lotte took the stage at her cue, her bared midriff admired by most of the men in the audience. She noticed Jack's grin of appreciation and his wink as she danced. She also made certain that the new man she had noticed had not vanished. He was still there but had moved from one of the wooden bar stools to a small empty table by the stage door, nursing his lager.

Lotte would be making sure he did not slip behind that curtain in search of Audrey if he was the threat. Even if that meant she had to dive off the stage and tackle him.

Lotte's jewelery jingled as she continued to move, hips flicking side to side, making the coins sewn into her hip scarf match the rhythm. The audience picked up the beat as she stomped her feet, many of them calling out to her as she shimmied and bent over backwards for them, quite literally.

Lotte finished and held her final pose, one hand up toward the sky, the other brushing the ground as she bent over. She looked out the corner of her eye, glad to see that the stranger had remained for her performance.

Back off stage, she changed into less revealing clothing and returned to her alcove to read cards for the remainder of the evening. Once the women were finished performing, the wrestling match would follow, which meant the lady companions in the audience often got bored and came to seek other distraction. Audrey was helping to deliver drinks and clearing tables, which meant Lotte could not see her so well from the alcove, so she was relieved each time she glimpsed her friend.

Lotte had finished with one woman and her questions about the fidelity of the married man she was dating. He wasn't faithful to anyone, but Lotte had sent her away smiling as per what she was meant to do. Lotte pulled the cards back in and was surprised when the new stranger she had seen entered the alcove.

"What are you supposed to be doing?" he asked.

"For just one dollar, I will read the cards and answer a question. For two, I will tell you your fortunes."

"That's a lot of money."

"If you are not able to pay..." Lotte began to reply with her usual response to that comment, but she trailed off. She wanted to read his cards, for in them she might get a hint of whether he was the threat to Audrey or not.

"I can pay," the man replied brusquely. He sat down across from Lotte, looking ridiculously big in the small chair that usually held much daintier clients. He pulled two dollars from his jacket pocket and set them down on the table.

"What is your name?" Lotte asked him once he was settled.

"If you know all, shouldn't you know that already?"

People often responded to her question in a similar fashion, the few men that came to see her often sneering and rude. This man seemed to be teasing her, an easy smile on his face.

Lotte shook her head. "I know only what the cards tell me, and they do not have alphabet enough to spell out names, especially long ones."

He laughed at that. "Fair enough, I am Teddy Stanway."

"Nice to meet you, Teddy. If you would please to pick up the deck of cards and shuffle them around as you wish, then place them in three piles in front of me."

"Why three piles?"

"Past, present, and future," Lotte explained, gesturing for him to pick up the Rider-Waite deck. It belonged to Sonja's parents who were both known to be part of the Spiritualist Society that many said practised the occult. It was different from the packs that Lotte had learned to read from with her father's mother, but it did the job.

Teddy looked at some of the pictures on the cards once he picked up the back. He was clearly curious but did not know what to make of them. Lotte watched him shrug to himself before he shuffled them clumsily. He made three uneven piles on the table which he pushed towards Lotte, messing up the tablecloth. Lotte smiled and moved the cards, smoothing out the velvet as she did.

She pulled four cards from the first pack and laid them down to look like a cross. "You have worked hard all your life, not a lot of time for joy or play, yet you have found a great deal of contentment in it. More recently, grief has visited you, leaving a large hole in your life. A mentor, but not your father. I want to say it is your uncle who has recently passed away. And with all you lost in it, you gained as well."

Lotte looked up from the cards to find Teddy staring at her, slack-jawed. "I am right, yes?"

"How?"

"This is what the cards tell me." Lotte knew she was breaking the rules to do such a serious reading, but she had to know this man.

She turned over the next lot of cards and set them into their positions in the spread. These ones did not paint him so well.

"You are lost and full of anger. This anger turns to violence, quite often in fact. You wish to punish people, but not all people."

Lotte looked at the man across the table and wondered if he might be the killer from the paper, punishing the women he saw perhaps as sinful. While some of the victims had been well-reputed ballerinas and singers, all had been women who took to the stage, and some pious people did not believe that was acceptable. It was hard to imagine; he did not seem so dangerous as he sat there, but perhaps even Jack the Ripper had been a charming and quiet man.

Teddy did not make eye contact this time as she regarded him.

Lotte slid four cards from the third pile and added them to the table, she had to press her lips together so she did not gasp as she looked at them.

Death, blood, destruction. Lotte was convinced by these cards that this was the dangerous man she needed to keep Audrey away from. She could perhaps do that, but she could hardly have him taken off the streets and locked up because of what the cards told her. No, she needed proof that he was a killer.

Lotte looked back up with a fake smile on her face. She was so good at faking it after months of practising while reading the cards and lying.

"Your old life will fall away to make room for you to rebuild a new life, the one you were destined for." It was definitely an interpretation of the same cards, but given what Lotte had decided, it was not one she could believe.

**

Lotte stepped outside Ziggy Rose, the cold hitting her after spending so long so warm within. She made a noise that might have been meant to resemble a word but did not, not in any way. Teddy laughed, and she turned, narrowing her eyes as she looked at him. "It is cold."

"Hardly. You can't even see your breath. Perfectly mild evening."

"You say as you button up your coat."

Teddy shrugged. "I have been advised that it is poor form to wander the streets with one's coat unbuttoned and simply not done in polite society."

"Really?" Lotte had never heard that, but then again, she only entertained polite society. She was not part of it. Besides, she was often cold, so if she was needing a coat, odds were, it was buttoned all the way up and she could not cause offence.

"It is true, my neighbours were most shocked when I went for a walk with my coat billowing around me. It was most unbecoming of my new station."

Lotte had to smile at the look on Teddy's face. He was trying to be pompous, and he just did not suit it. Like much it seemed of the rich life. It was hard to think he was a dangerous killer at times. Lotte had spent the last two nights having conversations with him to try to find out more about him and any viable information she could use to get him locked up before he could harm Audrey. She had learned nothing to help.

"What in name of the heavens is this?" Jack appeared at the corner of the building and stormed over to Lotte, his large hand wrapping around her small wrist firmly, too firmly. He tugged her away from Teddy and closer to him. "What do you think you are doing?"

"I am speaking with one of the customers who happened to be leaving at the same time as me," Lotte replied, perplexed by the anger in Jack's tone. He was glaring at her with such malice as if he had caught her in the arms of another man, rather than standing next to one having a pleasant conversation about the weather.

"You are not leaving together?"

Lotte shook her head. "No, we are not."

Teddy looked uncomfortable and tipped his hat. "Uh, I will leave you to the rest of your night. Good evening to you both."

He did not wait for them to return his farewell but walked away from them. Lotte noticed he stopped just around the corner. She could still see his arm and part of his face. She was not sure if he remained to watch how her encounter with Jack went or if he was waiting for Audrey to leave. She was not going to call out to him right now to ask, not while Jack still held her by the wrist in such a fashion.

"Will you please let go of me, Jack. You are hurting my arm."

Jack looked down at her wrist but did not let go. He looked back into her eyes. "Tell me you were not going home with him?"

"Why on earth would I be going home with him?" she asked, looking completely surprised. Lotte could not understand where this was coming from. She had denied Jack a kiss on their first evening out together, making him well aware of the kind of woman she was and what she expected from a potential suitor. It seemed ludicrous that he would now assume she would go home with another man. "Please let go of me, it is cold, and I am tired and wish to go home."

"Of course. I shall accompany you home," Jack replied. He moved his grip on her arm and placed hers around his, as if they were walking together. Yet there was nothing carefree and easy about the gesture. He was still holding on to her too tight.

"Jack, please, if you cannot treat me gently, I truly do not want you walking me home." Lotte was too tired to remember her manners right now, and she twisted around to pull herself free of Jack's hold. She gave him a disgusted look. "If you can recall how to treat a lady, you may call on me tomorrow as we planned. If you insist on acting like a jealous ninny, you can stay home."

She began to walk away from him and down the street towards her own home which was only two blocks away. She was surprised by her outburst, especially to someone of his status, but the pain in her wrist had spurred her words.

He quickly followed and got in her path.

"Lotte, forgive me." He took his hat off and held it to his chest. "I do not know what came over me. I saw you with that man and I lost my head. A jealous ninny, indeed."

"You hardly have cause to be jealous, and I do not get upset with the way I see other women drape themselves all over you each night you come to the show."

"I am sorry, it must be the hot-headedness the Astor family are known for. I truly do like you, Miss de Vries, and I am afraid I could not bear the thought of you being stolen away by another man from my grasp."

Lotte was touched by his candid words. She had never imagined a man like Jack might feel so deeply for her, especially after only a few weeks. Perhaps she could forgive his jealous idiocy. After all, it was only because he cared about it. She sighed and nodded.

"Very well, you may walk me home."

As she took Jack's arm, she glanced back and could not see Teddy Stanway lurking any longer. That was a relief. Audrey should be fine.

**

Jack did not call on her the next morning as he had planned, but she did receive a bouquet of flowers delivered by a young boy who looked thrilled when Lotte gave him a few coins for his trouble. The flowers took over the dining table, and both Audrey and Sonja gushed over them as much as Lotte did. A small note was attached. Jack had business to attend to but would see her in the evening. Business always seemed to prevent him from calling on her for lunch.

Lotte wove a carnation into her hair before the three women left together to walk to the theatre. They had cleaning duties to take care of before they set up for the first show. It was Friday, so there would be the lunch crowd, which the singers would entertain, followed by a matinée show in the mid-afternoon. Then dinner would begin to be served in the early evening, and the show would begin by eight. Lotte was only doing the matinée show today. She would do her card readings when they reopened until the evening show started, and then she would be free to leave after that for her dinner with Jack.

Cleaning and set up went quickly, and soon Lotte was seated in her alcove in full costume with her cards. Friday lunch and afternoon were often attended by older gentlemen and their wives, so Lotte was usually very busy as the wives came to have their fortunes read and talk together. These women certainly knew how to gossip, and their claws were sharp when it came to people they did not like. Luckily, Lotte always seemed to make them happy, most likely because she always told them what they wanted to hear.

"Lotte, sweet girl, wonderful news. You were right about the good news. Once we return home, Madam Maria Santé will be holding a séance at my house. Can you believe it!"

Lotte smiled as Elizabeth Spielberg took a seat. She and her husband were visiting their holiday home in Astoria for a month, and she was in every other day for readings from Lotte. She was part of the Spiritualist Society along with Sonja's parents, the Janssens. The Spielberg's were one of the leading members, so it was hardly surprising that she would have been selected for the séance. She had been talking about the coming visit by Madam Santé all week, therefore Lotte had not been going out on a limb much in telling her to expect news.

Several other women, including Sonja's mother, crowded around, and they began to talk about the event and what spirits Mrs Spielberg and Mrs Janssen would be wishing to communicate with. Lotte was simply decoration at this point, so she let her mind, and her eyes, wander. She noticed Teddy Stanway had joined them for lunch and was currently chatting with Audrey. Lotte watched every part of their interaction, but Teddy did nothing untoward, and Audrey soon left his side to talk to other guests.

Teddy noticed Lotte looking his way and gave her a smile, lifting his glass in salute. Lotte nodded back, a small nod, before she returned her gaze to the ladies chatting in front of her. Perhaps she could get to chat with him again. He still had not let anything slip that might help Lotte in her investigation nor in making certain that Audrey remained alive.

As if the fates had chosen to listen to her thoughts, when the crowd thinned down with the serving of the second course of lunch, Teddy made his way over and took the empty seat across the table.

"Do you wish to know more from the cards?" Lotte asked.

"Actually, I wished to make sure you were well after your encounter with your fiancé last night."

"Fiancé?" Lotte shook her head and laughed. "No, we are not that involved."

"Oh, I assumed…"

"A fair assumption, but we are not, and I am fine. Mister Astor apologised for making assumptions."

"Astor?"

"Yes, as in Astoria. That family. I should not truly talk about it, but he is the recently discovered child of John Astor the Fourth who died on the Titanic. Jack has been taken into the family and is currently staying with his Aunt Carrie."

"Is that so?" Teddy remarked. He had a look on his face that was unreadable by Lotte, perhaps something akin to confusion. Or perhaps it was surprise. "He does not look anything like his father."

"You knew his father?"

"I have seen pictures," Teddy replied. He rose from his seat and looked out around the room behind them. Lotte followed his gaze. She could see Audrey milling about by the bar. "I should go."

"You do not need to," Lotte replied, eager to keep him away from Audrey. His whole demeanour had changed, and there was something worrisome about it.

"No, I should leave you to your job."

"Perhaps we could talk again later?"

Teddy's gaze swung back to Lotte. "What would your Jack say about that?"

Lotte laughed that off. "I am allowed to speak with whomever I wish. And I would like to speak to you some more."

Teddy seemed surprised by her words, but they made him smile and seem more relaxed again. "I would like that. Are you performing this afternoon?"

"I am."

"Perhaps I might speak with you after the show then," Teddy said. He moved to touch his hat, only to realise that he was not wearing one. Hats and coats were taken on entry. He chuckled slightly and touched his hand to his chest.

Lotte smiled. If she did not know what the cards had told her, she would find Teddy quite a sweet and charming gentleman. "I will make myself available then."

"I look forward to it," Teddy replied and then left. Men so often seemed to have more than one side to them, a hidden face that was often seen too late. It was hard to account that Teddy Stanway had two such opposing sides to him. Perhaps there was simply something wrong in his mind and soul, a schism, as if two separate men lived within the one. She watched him walk away, waiting for him to return to Audrey, but he took a seat at the bar, and his attention was on the stage as the entertainment began. Theresa had a lovely voice.

**

The afternoon show passed quickly with only a minor incident with the trapeze act, which thankfully did not lead to serious injuries. Soon after, Lotte was changed and ready to enjoy her downtime before they opened again for dinner. Teddy was waiting outside; his coat was buttoned up, and he held a scarf in his hands. "I thought we might stroll down by the water, and you might need this if you were cold."

Lotte smiled. "How very thoughtful of you, Mister Stanway."

"Your friend with the dark eyes was amazing this afternoon, I did not know people could bend like that."

He was talking about Audrey as he reached forward and draped the scarf around Lotte's neck, a liberty she might not have let him take if it weren't for the topic. "Yes, Audrey is very bendy. It terrifies me sometimes."

"I admit I felt an odd sensation, almost a worry that she would not be able to untangle herself and get back out of the container. Shall we?"

He had twisted the scarf around and was standing very close to Lotte. For a moment, there was a feeling of energy that passed between them, and had it not been for the threat to Audrey, Lotte would have sighed. Teddy stepped back and offered his arm which Lotte took.

Her fingers brushed the skin of the back of his hand, and an image came into Lotte's mind, much like happened with the cards on a good day. She saw Teddy full of rage and splattered in blood.

It had to prove that he was the monster intent on harming Audrey. Quite suddenly, Lotte felt very foolish to have agreed to go for a walk with him. For all she knew, he might do something to her while they were out of sight of others. Still, she had sworn to do what it took to save Audrey, and if she ended up murdered, perhaps Teddy would move on from this place and the attention her death would bring to him.

"Tell me about yourself, Mister Stanway."

He turned his head and gave her a cheeky grin. "Your cards did not tell you all?"

"Oh, they told me plenty, but I wish to know the little things. Are you a local to Astoria?"

Teddy shook his head. "No, I spent time here growing up visiting my Uncle at one of his houses, but I was born and raised just outside of Philadelphia. We had a farm, and I helped my mother run it after my father died."

There was a pang of sadness in his voice, Lotte had a feeling it was not for the lost father but for the mother who was now gone. Lotte had picked that up in the cards. His mother had died not so long ago, and then his uncle had followed. His grief had brought him here, that and an inheritance.

That inheritance was why he was now part of the high society, and yet he was still not part of it.

"My parents died when I was young," Lotte said, unsure why she was opening up to a man who she had just seen after a murder in her mind. She looked down at the ground as they walked. He seemed to pick up on her unease and continued to talk about the farm and his life on it.

The afternoon was overcast but still bright enough to see that they both cast shadows. Vampires could not do that, Lotte mused, could they? Or was it that they did not have reflections in mirrors? Lotte had almost forgotten thinking the killer was a vampire, perhaps because Teddy had none of the characteristics she imagined such creatures had. His skin was deeply tanned, not deathly, or rather, undeadly pale. He was a muscular man with broad shoulders. Vampires were meant to be tall and thin, with fingers like weathered twigs and nails like talons. His hair was brown, lightened in places by too much time in the sun, it was not long and black. Plus, there was the fact that, overcast or not, Teddy was strolling with her during the day. Lotte was quite certain that sunlight was a definite no-no for vampires.

Still, just because he was not a real vampire did not mean he was not the killer, nor did it mean he was not a threat to sweet Audrey. One did not have to be the serial killer from the papers to end up taking a young woman's life.

"You are very quiet, Miss De Vries," Teddy said, glancing at her.

Lotte quickly looked away, not wanting him to realise that she had been studying him as they walked. "I am sorry. I was wondering why you come to Ziggy Rose. It does not seem like it would be your type of establishment."

Teddy shrugged, Lotte caught the movement out of the corner of her eye.

"I was lonely."

Lotte frowned at the implication, her hands tensing at her sides. "Well, we are not that kind of establishment, Mister Stanway. We entertain yes, but we do not help men with their... loneliness."

Teddy came to an abrupt stop and turned to look at Lotte with utter horror. "I did not mean. That is. I was hoping to become more acceptable to the others by frequenting the same places."

"Oh," Lotte murmured, releasing the little fists her hands had made. "I see."

And she did. He had come into money and the position others were born into, and they did not give him the same respect for it. He hoped to forge friendships with his new peers, not get friendly with the performers. Lotte could understand that, and she also understood how hard that must be. Many of those who came to the show looked down their noses at the staff, and the way they gossiped about each other showed a distinct lack of respect for even their peers. It had to be very hard for Teddy to enter their circles.

Teddy had a sadness in his eyes as she looked up at him that made her, at that moment, forget he might be intent on killing one of her closest friends. Lotte softly touched Teddy's hand. Her fingers were gentle as they brushed the back of it. "I am sorry they have made you feel so unwelcome."

Teddy beamed a smile at her. It was so brilliant that Lotte had to look away, suddenly bashful to be here with him, to have touched him. He was kind about her embarrassment and did not push further, or even mention the act. Instead, he turned and resumed their stroll.

"You are very kind. Most of the others at Ziggy Rose are not very interested in talking with me. Almost as if they too realise

I do not belong. One of the others was, I think you said her name was Aubrey, the bendy one."

"Audrey. You seemed quite taken with her when you spoke."

"I did?" He sounded genuinely surprised. "Her talent is definitely quite unusual and interesting, to be sure, but it is not she who I invited to walk with me."

Lotte felt her heart quicken and her stomach tense at his words and the glance he gave her. She was quite certain that she blushed. "You did not wish to use me to gain more knowledge of her?"

Teddy shook his head. "I do not believe in using others. Another reason I do not seem to fit in with those visiting their holiday homes this month."

"I thought…" Lotte murmured, unable to vocalise just what she had thought. Teddy was seeming less and less like a threat to anyone, let alone Audrey. Despite the violence and the image she had seen, he simply seemed like a lovely and lonely man.

Teddy stopped and turned to Lotte. He placed a hand on her arm to stop her walking and turn her to face him. "I think you are quite wonderful, Miss de Vries. You have shown more kindness than most."

"Mister Stanway," Lotte stammered his name, flustered by the way he was staring at her and more so by the fact that she liked it. "You barely know me. And Jack, that is, Mister Astor…"

"How much do you know of Jack Astor?"

"A great deal more than I know about you," Lotte replied more pompously than she intended. She did know Jack better and she was very fond of him. So, she should not have these giddy feelings inside right now from being with Teddy and him smiling as he was at her. She turned away from him and looked out across the water, watching the caps of the waves as they broke before they reached the land. The wind rose suddenly and blew strands of Lotte's hair free of her up-do. It felt like her hair was coming undone, as she was herself.

"Miss de Vries, Lotte, I do not think you know him so well. I think he is purposely misleading you."

Lotte swung around, her own feelings of guilt making her turn unkind. "You think you can speak ill of him in hopes of turning my head? How dare you be so presumptuous? Good day, Mister Stanway." Lotte felt incredibly ashamed that she was alone with this man, that she was enjoying her time with him. Jack had accused her last night of being inappropriately involved with Teddy, and here she was, proving him right. He would be so angry with her right now if he knew. She could picture his anger so clearly.

She turned away and lifted her skirts, running from Teddy as if she might run from the things she was feeling too.

She had been so certain she needed to spend time with Teddy for Audrey's sake and had instead led him on in ways she should not have. She had never really thought what it might result in. Jack had clearly seen what she had not, a man who wanted more from her than a conversation about the weather. She had been fixated on seeing the killer. She had forgotten to see him as a man.

Lotte was equal parts relieved and disappointed when she reached her apartment and Teddy had not followed her. She let herself inside and spent her remaining break time lying on her bed with a pillow over her face, muffling her voice as she berated her own foolishness.

Just on sunset, Lotte left the apartment and made her way back to work. Teddy was waiting for her just outside the rear entrance. She gave him a tight smile, not wanting to offend a paying patron of Ziggy Rose. "Good evening, Mister Stanway. I hope you enjoy tonight's show."

Teddy touched her elbow. Lotte looked down at it pretending to be offended by the touch. He did not remove his hand.

"Please, I need to talk to you. Jack Astor is not who he claims. You must listen to me."

"What you need is of little consequence, and I must do nothing when it comes to you. What I must do is go and prepare myself."

"Lotte, please."

Teddy spoke her name with such an impassioned plea that she finally looked up at him. The look on his face made her sigh and surrender.

"Fine. You may come and speak to me once I am seated in the booth. You have the length of one reading to explain yourself." She could not believe she was relenting, but the way his eyes held hers seemed to undo her. Lotte realised that for the first time she was looking at him without the bias that had clouded her judgments. She let her instincts truly take his measure. He was a lovely and lonely man who looked at her with the eyes of someone who cared. He cared, without expectation or demand. He simply cared.

Lotte hurried away inside, her guilt resurfacing because she very much liked the fact that Teddy Stanway cared about her. What kind of woman did that make her?

She changed her gown and accessorised to look the part of the tarot card reader before she made her way from the dressing room backstage to her alcove in the corner. Teddy did not come to her booth immediately, but she saw him watching, waiting until no other was in line to hurry him along.

Lotte also kept her eye out for Jack's arrival, knowing he was coming to take her out for dinner. She was grateful that Jack had not arrived for her yet, which just made her feel guilty again.

Teddy came over from the bar and sat down when her table emptied. He handed over two dollars, even though Lotte had not told him he had to pay. He took the cards and shuffled them again, barely looking at them as he held her gaze. "I live next door to a woman who is a close friend of Carrie Astor. I had met her several times since I arrived, and I went to see her again this morning. Jack Astor's claims are false. She has no bastard nephew staying with her."

He split the deck into three parts and set them down in front of Lotte. She turned cards over, her hands moving in a well-rehearsed motion, her eyes still holding his.

"Perhaps I misheard him, and he is staying elsewhere. Perhaps a hotel," she replied, searching for reasonable excuses for Teddy's information.

"No. Lotte, you must understand, there is no illegitimate son of John Astor. The man is a fiction."

"That is impossible."

"He is a conman. He is…"

"No," Lotte cut him off, "that is not possible."

She tore her gaze away from his brown eyes and looked down at the cards she had laid out and gasped. Fear immediately gripped her. "Audrey…"

She had not even checked in on her friend this evening. She had not thought of the threat; her thoughts had been consumed by Teddy. And now, laid out on the tablecloth, were the exact cards she had pulled for Audrey the other night.

Lotte stood up quickly, knocking the small table over. Her cards and the velvet tablecloth spilt across the carpet, but Lotte did not care to pick them back up. She ran from the booth, skirts lifted wickedly high so she could move faster. She rushed by the stage door curtain and ran into the dressing room. There was only one woman there. "Fleur, where is Audrey?"

Fleur gave her a smirking look that was full of gleeful malice. "Oh, did you not hear? She stepped out with Jack; it seems you are not so special after all."

"Go swallow your teeth," Lotte spat back, in no mood for Fleur's usual pettiness. She ran back out of the room and out the rear door of the building, sprinting down the alley with her skirts bunched up around her thighs, looking around to see any hint of Audrey. As she approached the end of the brick building, the door of a black Ford parked along there opened. Lotte realised it was idling, not parked.

"I have been waiting for you, darling."

Lotte recognised the voice and moved closer to see into the vehicle. Jack was sitting in the driver's seat with Audrey, and he had a knife to her throat. Her mouth was bound, her eyes wide with terror. It seemed Teddy was right; Jack Astor was not who he claimed to be but it was so much more than he imagined. Lotte saw the blood and wounds on Audrey's neck and the blood on Jack's lips.

"Get in the car, Lotte, and perhaps I will let your friend live out the night."

Lotte did not stop to argue or beg Jack. She walked around the car and got in. She had been intent on keeping Audrey safe all this time. She was not going to stop now she had found the real danger. Lotte closed the door and waited. Jack grinned at her with bloodstained pointed teeth, and she wondered how she had not seen it before.

The handsome and charming gentleman who was so pale-skinned. He never came to see her for lunch even though he promised, too busy with the business he claimed. Come to think of it, Lotte was not sure she had ever seen him eat nor drink. Yes, she had seen him with a cup in his hand, but she could not recall seeing him empty it.

Jack kept Audrey in his lap and began to drive, still holding the handle of his knife between his fingers. They picked up speed as they drove down the main road, the driver's door banging as it flapped, still open. To Lotte's horror, Jack suddenly released the knife and pushed Audrey off his lap and right out of the car. He pulled the door closed, and Lotte turned to watch Audrey bouncing on the road as they continued to speed away.

Lotte twisted in her seat to look out the back of the car, and she saw Audrey sit up on the road. She was clearly alive, if injured, and that was a small relief to Lotte.

Lotte twisted back in her seat in time to see a small wooden paddle come at her face. It connected painfully, and she lost consciousness.

**

Lotte woke up in a small wooden chair. Her wrists were tied behind her back with a thick rope. Strangely, that was the only way she had been secured while she was unconscious. Lotte looked around her surrounds. She was in a room in a house, a room that looked like no one had lived in it for quite some time. She was in a dining room, sitting where the table should be. There was a hutch cabinet against one wall. It was large, and Lotte could see there was still glassware sitting behind the glass doors of the top of the hutch. Against the other wall stood several china cabinets with pretty figurines sitting on top of them. Inside the cabinets was all the family china, along with trinkets that looked like they were from foreign lands. This was obviously the house of a well to do family, not as wealthy as Jack Astor had claimed to be but definitely better off than Lotte's family had been.

All the cabinets and the objects on top of them were thick with dust, and there were sizable spiders' webs draped between the ceiling at the ornaments on the china cabinets. No sign of the spiders though, thankfully. Perhaps they had not had any fresh food with no family present and taken their web-spinning elsewhere. Lotte hoped so; she could not abide spiders.

The right side of her face pulsed with pain from where Jack had hit her. Thankfully, while it hurt, it was not incapacitating. She twisted her wrists in the rope. It was rough and painful, but she thought perhaps she might be able to get herself free of it. She froze as Jack entered the room. He had changed his clothes again and looked every inch the rich man she had become involved in. He adjusted the ends of his shirt sleeves beneath his jacket and looked up at her.

"Oh good, you have finally woken."

"You say that as if I have inconvenienced you by being unconscious when you are the one who hit me," Lotte replied, amazing herself at how even her tone was. She sounded as if she were conducting a normal conversation and not actually consumed by fear and anger. Lotte had learned at an early age that men often did not want to deal with an upset woman, and it could lead to a worse situation. Jack seemed like he might react worse if she were to become emotional. Vampire or human, he was clearly unstable, and Lotte wished she had seen it sooner rather than being charmed by him. She had noticed nothing, not even with his tantrum over Teddy.

Teddy. Surely Teddy had realised something had happened by now. But how would he or anyone know where to look for her when she had no idea where she even was?

"You left me little choice, misbehaving as you have been. You are mine, and yet I arrive to see you with that mutt again." Jack had raised his voice as he spoke and already seemed to be getting angry despite Lotte trying to sound calm.

"Mutt?"

"That one you assured me you had no interest in, and yet even now I can smell his stink on you."

"His stink on me?" Lotte might have been offended by the implication if she was not so confused. Teddy had barely touched her, nor her him, so how could she smell like him? Did Vampires have an incredibly heightened sense of smell to be able to detect even a small touch?

While Lotte believed in vampires, because her Oma had claimed to have met one and Oma never lied, she did not know much about them. Abraham Van Helsing might have been a Dutchman in the books, but the Dutch did not have many vampire stories to teach Lotte about them.

"Yes, I saw you when I arrived at the club in my motor car. You did not even notice me as he touched your arm."

"He touched my arm, so you kidnap me and hurt Audrey?"

"Audrey was simply to ensure your compliance. If she had not been there, I would have taken someone else."

Lotte stared at Jack. Audrey had not been an intended target at any point it seemed, but the cards...Lotte had been blinded by the cards with Teddy, completely misreading the situation with blinkers on. Unfortunately, it appeared she had done so in regards to the initial reading as well. Audrey had never been in any real danger. The cards had been for her. They had been trying to warn her of her own impending doom.

"Such a look of horror. I do love it, but it is not quite as I wished it," Jack said, studying her. He leaned back against the lower shelf of the hutch and smiled at Lotte. "You were meant to be quite in love with me. There is something so delicious about watching the love turn to terror. But you and your mutt have ruined my hard work."

Jack pushed off from the hutch and moved around behind Lotte. He leaned down and brushed his lips against the side of her neck. Lotte tensed, trying to pull away from him. Jack laughed. "Perhaps this shall be a new kind of pleasure. You will be the first to resist me."

His fingers slid under the shoulders of her dress. He pulled hard at the fabric, and both sides ripped under his extreme strength. He let go of the fabric, and it fell down her arms, leaving her shoulders and much of her upper torso on display. Lotte glanced down, relieved that her breasts, for the most part, were still hidden.

"You try to do anything to me, and I will bite you much harder than you did Audrey," Lotte replied, glaring even though he was behind her and could not see her. There was a part of her that wanted to burst into tears, to weep and to beg, but she had lived long enough to know that would not help her.

Jack moved around the chair and knelt down on the floor in front of her. He looked so handsome still, and yet somehow, the truth of his character shone forth and made him sickening to look at. He reached up and gently stroked his finger up and down her throat. "Bite all you wish, my lips and teeth and tongue shall be claiming every inch of your skin. Why should you not get to have some fun too? I am going to claim you completely, my darling Lotte. You women say no and claim to want no part in such activities, but deep down you crave for us to subjugate you."

"Is that so?"

"It is true. Even your God believes your bodies are made for us. You were, after all, made of man, for man. You are ours, and it makes you heated between your thighs when we take what is ours. It is why you perform; it is why you seek to glitter on stage for us to see you. You are like birds, prettily calling for a mate to claim you."

Lotte wished she could argue with his logic, but she had heard such things spouted at her before. Not the gross comments about between her thighs, but the comments about the ownership of women by the men in their lives. She knew women who had left Ziggy Rose, women of some independence, who had been completely dominated by their new husbands. Lotte had never believed it must be the case. She had seen the loving partnership between her parents before they had become sick.

"My God believes nothing of the sort. Nor my Goddess," Lotte retorted. Any God that might think women should be treated in such a way was not one worthy of Lotte's love, and she had been raised in more ancient beliefs. She had been raised to worship women who were Goddesses, who were warriors, who were powerful. The kind of women that would step on men like Jack and the others who thought as they did.

Lotte wished one might come and step on Jack now.

"A heathen? Well, aren't you more than I supposed when I first chose you?" Jack let his fingers trace over Lotte's collarbones as he smiled at her. He seemed delighted by her revelation, something that set him apart from most God-fearing folk. "Would you like to know why I chose you?"

"No, I would not," Lotte said, sneering at Jack. Her hands were incredibly sore right now, but she nearly had one free. "Perhaps you can instead tell me who you really are?"

"My name is John, but I do prefer Jack, I did not lie about that. It's so tiresome to try to remember different names. I did know John Astor on the Titanic. He died, I did not, and I saw an opportunity. People are so welcoming to a wealthy name."

Lotte hissed a breath as Jack's hand started to move lower on her chest. She was not going to let this happen to her. She yelped as she got her hand free and clutched the side of the chair with it. She moved her weight to her feet and pulled the chair from underneath her, clobbering Jack in the side of the face with it. He was so surprised, he did not react in time to stop her, and she ran out of the room, turning right in the hopes that this hallway might take her to a front door, or an easy exit.

"Grab her!" Jack yelled from the room.

Lotte realised then that they were not alone in the house. Two men and a woman appeared around her, one man behind her, the other man and woman in front of her, blocking her way. She charged at the ones in front of her. Her foot caught in her skirts which she had not taken the time to raise. She fell forward as she ran, straight into the man. Her shoulder connected with his stomach, knocking the air out of him.

The woman with him grabbed her by the shoulders and pulled her upwards. Lotte ducked her head as the woman went to hit her in the face. It was sore enough already from Jack knocking her out.

There was a loud growl outside. All three of them paused in motion as there came the loud sound of wood breaking. Lotte used the moment of distraction to get free of the woman's grasp. She sunk her teeth into the woman's hand. She screamed immediately, loosening her grip. Lotte pushed past her and turned away from the growling and wood breaking. She did not want to see what other monsters this house held. She just needed to find a window to break and get out.

She ran into a room and slammed the door shut, looking around to see what she could put against it. The room was almost completely dark, and Lotte could see very little. Instead, she pushed her back against the door, heels pressed into the floor to try and find a grip should anyone come at the door directly.

A moment later, the handle turned and the door flexed. Lotte held her place as it was pushed, but the second attempt to open it was successful. It was opened with such force that Lotte was thrown across the room. She landed awkwardly on her face, screaming in pain as the hard floor impacted her bruises.

Jack grabbed her and rolled her over, looming over her. He pushed her face to the side with one hand, the other on her shoulder as his body pinned her own. He was so strong, and Lotte could do little more than wriggle and kick her legs up in the air. He leaned down and bit her. She felt his sharp fangs enter her skin like the points of knives. Lotte screamed. She lifted her legs, trying to kick him in the back but could not even unbalance him.

Her eyes were growing more accustomed now in the dim light, and she saw the room held broken furniture. She was close to a broken table, a broken mirror, and torn linen. She got her arm free, and while she could not push Jack away, she tried to reach something, anything. She got her hand on a piece of the table, but the edges were too blunt for it to be a stake, and it was too light for her to do anything with it. She grabbed the linen and pulled, it sent the cracked mirror to the ground and shards of broken mirror scattered across the floor.

Desperate, Lotte grabbed one and with all her strength, drove it into Jack's face as he lapped at her blood.

The shard of mirror cut her hand up painfully, but she managed to lodge it into his eye. Jack fell back, howling in pain, and Lotte grabbed two more shards of mirror and with the two pointy ends, she returned the favour he had bestowed on her and pierced his neck. As he fell back, she grabbed the piece of table and when he hit the ground, she leapt on him, using the wood to push the mirror deep into his throat. He shuddered and went still, blood gushing from the wounds all over the floor.

Lotte fell off him, rolling away from the blood onto her knees. She pressed a now bloodied hand to her own neck wound and crawled one-handed out of the room. Feet approached her, and her heart sunk that she was still in danger. She looked up to find Teddy standing over her. His suit was soaked in blood and torn apart. His hair was longer and disheveled. He was every inch the monster she had seen in her mind when she had touched him by the shore.

"Found you." He dropped to his knees and pulled her to him, looking at her throat. "You hurt."

"I hurt," Lotte replied. "But, he is dead. Jack is dead. I killed him."

"Others too, others dead," Teddy replied with a nod. He sounded so simple, his voice rough and deep.

He picked her up easily and walked her out of the house. In the brighter moonlight outside, Lotte saw that his brown eyes shone almost gold.

He looked down at her and shrugged. "Not all monsters bad."

Lotte nodded. Not all monsters were bad, not all men were good, and the cards had been right about everything. Her hands shook violently as she curled against Teddy's hairy chest between the rips of his shirt.

Things were not always what they appeared, and maybe there was a reason that Stoker had chosen a Dutchman to be his vampire hunter. Perhaps it was in the blood of their people, a hidden skill. Lotte had killed her first vampire tonight, no mean feat. Perhaps she was meant for more than just reading cards and dancing for others. A woman had entered that building, a killer had exited.

Jack could not be the only one in the world. There had to be more dangerous vampires out there waiting to prey on other women, on women like Audrey.

A shiver ran through her body, and it was more than just for the cold and the blood lust. Lotte felt an instinctive certainty; her task was not finished yet. And perhaps the cards were right for Teddy too, perhaps he had found a new life. It seemed he was more than just a farmer or a rich man. The notion felt right even as Lotte thought it.

Lotte and Teddy - Vampire Hunters.

Jai Lefay

Jai Lefay lives in New Zealand writing Supernatural, Historic, & Fantasy Fiction, while running her own dance studio and performing in variety and burlesque shows. She is a Holistic Creatrix who can be found across the Internet as ThePrincessBard, empowering others to chase their own dreams.

Find her on-line at:

> http://theprincessbard.com/books-by-jai-lefay/

Support her Patreon at:

> https://www.patreon.com/theprincessbard.

She's also on social media at:

- Facebook: https://www.facebook.com/theprincessbard/

- Twitter: https://www.instagram.com/theprincessbard/

- Instagram: https://twitter.com/ThePrincessBard

The Shadows Breathe

By A.R. Reinhardt

The Shadows Breathe

She doesn't know that she's dead,
                                                      yet.

But that's normal. As normal as these situations can be. Hell isn't a place. It's a moment in time, the worst moment. And for people like her - for people like me - it's the last moment. That's where she is, now. In that shadowy place between the end of everything
                and the beginning of the
                                        rest.

I watch her from my place in the shadows, a silent witness to the way that she thrashes against the sheets, to the way that her blue lips open and close to make room for screams that no longer make a sound and to gasp for air that she can no longer breathe. Her eyes are white, pupils bleached to a hazy blue. I wonder if she's noticed that she can no longer see in colour, or if her attention is held entirely by the rusted chain that keeps her connected to the bed.

She thinks that the Man with the Dark Hat put it there. And she's right, in a way. He did, but not with his hands. Just his actions. Every step that he'd taken to bring her here, every single thing that he'd done to her, the last breath that he stole from her lungs, it all led to this. To a rusted chain, to a messy bed, to the spirit with silent screams and tear stained cheeks.

And to
        me.

But **the**y won't know that until it's too late.

I hear the front door open, and so does she, I can tell by the way that her thrashing stops, all at once, her mouth closing and her eerie, dead eyes widen. She's still afraid of him, even now, still afraid because she doesn't know that he's already done the worst that he can to her, that there's nothing else for him to take.

I remember that fear, as sharply and as clearly as I had felt it when my eyes first opened to this grey world beyond the one that I had known, and my tongue tastes metallic with that cloying flavour as I finally step out from my place in the shadows.

The Man With the Dark Hat doesn't hear my footsteps, but she does. She turns her head, slowly, and her eyes meet mine. Her blue lips, dry and cracked, form a perfect "O" of surprise and tears, black as ink, well up in her eyes.

"Help me," she whispers, her voice scratching and cold, like dry autumn leaves scraping against the sidewalk. "Please, please help me."

I raise a finger to my lips, bidding her to be quiet, and she closes her mouth immediately, watching me even as her fingers scrape against the chain that's holding her.

I keep to the shadows as I slip from the bedroom to the hall. Pictures line these walls, frozen smiles and lifeless eyes all framed in gold. Relics of a family that The Man With the Dark Hat used to have and refuses to let go of, just as he refuses to let go of the girl that is chained to his bed.

> I think men like him keep these reminders out of spite, not love.

> I think men like him decorate their lair with everything they lost to justify what they'll
> > take.

I slip from the hall to the living room, where the man stands. His coat, wet from the rain, is tossed carelessly to the floor, and he kicks off his muddy shoes, splattering the wall with the traces of where he's been. And he shuffles from the doorway to the kitchen, opening the fridge and rifling around for cans of beer and cold leftovers.

He won't go to his room. Not yet. And even if he did, he wouldn't see her. He can't feel the weight of the life that he's torn through and destroyed. He knows nothing of chains or hell. He is a black hole, a dark pit, endless in his consumption of what surrounds him. Never full or satisfied.

He finishes rifling through his fridge and returns to his living room. I watch him as he goes, sticking to him like a shadow. He whistles a tune to fill the silence and then settles down onto a stained armchair and switches on the television to watch the news with anxious eyes, waiting for proof that he's gotten away with it. He will feel no relief when he finds out that he has. Only validation, seeing it as proof that he is smarter
    cleverer better than everyone, including the police.

It will only make him hungry,
                        again.

The voices of the television drone on. They talk about the weather. About sports. About the good deeds of men who are not like the man who sits in front of me. And then, finally, they move on. A special report about a missing girl. The television frames her like the pictures in his hall, a moment in time captured. And he jeers when the reporter says that there are no leads, no evidence, no suspects. It's been days, and the family is still begging whoever took their daughter to return her, safely.

He takes a triumphant sip of his beer, smugness radiating off of him in waves. He thinks he's
>   won.

And that's when I press the palm of my hand against the
>   television.

I can feel it hiss and spit and spark under my touch. The droning voice of the reporter is swallowed by a sea of static. It startles the man, who chokes on his bite of food. He coughs angrily and picks up the remote, trying to change the channel. It doesn't work.

"What the
>   hell?"

I press the palm of my hand harder against the screen until the bulb inside of the television bursts. The sound cracks through the silence and frightens him. He trips over himself, falling back into his chair and kicking over his beer in the process. It tips over, lazily glug

        glug

                glugging

                        out.

"Shit!" He swears, picking the mostly empty can back up and setting it back on the table. He shakes the liquid off of his hand and kicks the table, blaming it for the mess. "Fucking bulb must have -"

Click.

Click.

Click.

The lights are the next thing to go. The lamp that sits on the end table next to the couch, the lights in the kitchen. They all fall to the seizing hands of the shadows, all at once. He looks up at the sound, wetting his lips with his tongue. He's nervous, now.

"...Musta been a power surge," He says, to himself. "Blew the fuse. Blew the bulbs or whatever. Where did I leave those fucking flashlights?"

He talks to himself to distract from the silence. And from the fear that makes beads of sweat appear at his hairline. He wipes them away with the back of his hand and lumbers to the kitchen, yanking drawers open and then slamming them closed, again, when he doesn't find what he's looking for. He swears and marches to the bedroom.

I'm already there without moving from the living room, drawn to the space like a magnet. The girl is still there, still chained to the bed and cries inky tears when she sees him, but his gaze slides right over her. He only sees empty sheets and rumpled blankets. He goes to the nightstand beside where the girl is chained and yanks open drawers until he finds a flashlight.

He presses the switch, and it illuminates briefly before the shadows swallow it whole.

The light sputters out, and he swears and stomps his feet like an enraged child. And the girl still cries, her matted hair hanging in her face.

"Help me. Help me. Help me." She begs, over and over again.

It's
    time.

The man throws his flashlight across the room. It collides with the wall and falls in pieces and, in the moments after, there is only the sound of his laboured breathing. I watch as he rubs his hands against his face and tries to calm himself back down. He starts back for the door, muttering something about a spare in the hall closet with his camping gear, but the door slams shut before he can make it out.

The man yelps with fear and flails backward, falling halfway onto the bed and halfway onto the floor, his feet kicking the base of a full-length mirror that stands propped up beside the bed, another silent witness to the horrors that took place here.

He is staring ahead with crazed eyes. His lips move, silently, urging himself to speak more lies. To convince himself that everything is fine.

He finally scrambles back to his feet, pulling himself up by gripping the sheets and using them to carry his weight upward. He looks around the room, searching for another way out. And it's then and only then that he finally sees her. The girl, the life that he ended, still on his bed. He shouts and tumbles back to the floor, kicking his feet and swinging his fists at an invisible enemy, knocking the mirror over onto its side. Spiderweb cracks run through its surface, distorting what it reflects.

"No!" He shouts, his voice shaking. "NO! It can't be you, I - I got rid of
    you!"

She's gone when he looks again, unseen by his eyes, but I can see the understanding dawning in her expression, the final piece clicking into place when she realizes that she is dead. She no longer begs me to help her. She doesn't have to. If life is an endless pursuit of knowledge, then death is a final understanding, and she realizes what I'd known the whole time.

The mirror begins to
    shake.

The man pushes back away from it, his eyes wild and nearly bugging out of his head, desperately shifting to and fro from the other pieces of furniture, searching for evidence of a freak earthquake. But everything else stands still and silent while the mirror continues to shake and shift. I am both watching and crawling, as fractured as the glass in the mirror, a silent witness to his fate and the cause.

I push forward, and the glass pushes with me, an iridescent bubble. Smooth surface pressed and stretched thin like elastic around my hollow eyes and gasping mouth. I push
    And push until the bubble gives away. It does not
        burst,

I just slide through. A contorted body, a mass of awkward limbs and living shadows. I struggle to right myself, gasping like the girl had, for air that does not belong to me. It is painful to be in this living realm; this space that does not want to house me. The colours are too vibrant, every noise too loud. My joints crack and pop as I drag myself across the floor.

    I
        Rise.

Towering over the man, with limbs too long and a mouth too wide. I used to smile in the face of their fear, but now I just stare, my own eyes white with milky-blue pupils. My neck is at an odd angle, bruises in the shapes of the fingers that had dug into my skin so long ago.

"You're not the girl," He says, voice shaking with relief. "You're not
        her."

                No, I'm
                      not.

                      I am
                          worse.

I can no longer see the girl on the bed, not in this mortal realm. But I know where her body would be, and I can still hear her whispers, in my head, begging me to help.

"You're not the girl." The man says, again, a cold realization washing over him. "Am I dreaming? What are you? What do you want?"

I don't answer him. I don't think I could, my throat is too damaged to speak. But I move forward, feet not quite touching the ground.

"Is this about her?" He asks, pleading now. "I'm sorry. I'm so sorry. I didn't mean to. I couldn't help myself! I'm sick! It's not my fault, I can't control...please! Please, I won't ever do it again! God, oh Jesus, what are you? Leave me alone!"

He is right about one thing. He won't ever do this
again.

I finally
        smile
                and lunge at
                        him.

He can't move away from me, petrified by his own fear. My hand touches his chest and then slides through, fingers wrapping around his heart and squeezing lightly. I snuff out his life as easily as I had the lights in his home. The light leaves his eyes and there is only silence.

※※※

I am myself again when I see the girl. Crossing back over to the land where I belong is easier and less painful than dragging myself into the land of the living. Her chain is gone, and she sits on the edge of the bed. Her eyes are no longer white with blue pupils. They are warm and brown, now.

"Thank you," She whispers to me, rubbing at her wrist where the cuff had once been. There is no pain after its removal, no marks left behind. She is just admiring her own freedom. She is brighter without fear... and growing brighter still.

She is free. There is nothing holding her here. But she reaches out for me, her hand grasping at mine, but I pull away before she can touch.

"Aren't you coming?"

She thinks I am her guardian angel. And I finally speak to her.

"No," I say, my voice cold and scratchy, like autumn leaves scraping against the sidewalk. "I cannot follow you there."

She is free. But I'm not. I sit there, on the edge of the bed with her, and I watch as she's bathed in the soft, warm light. She's gone when the room grows dark again, and I rub my wrist, mirroring her actions from just minutes ago. I broke my own chain a long time ago, but that's not what keeps me here, out of the light. It's the spirits like her, who can't free themselves as I did.

And as long as there are people like her, I'll always belong to the
> shadows.

A.R. Reinhardt

A.R Reinhardt is a non-binary author who lives in Massachusetts with their girlfriend and two sons, and spends their days writing Supernatural, Horror, and Urban Fantasy Fiction and sharing that fact with literally anyone who will listen.

Night of the Beast

By Cassy Crownover

Corinth, Mississippi – June 12, 1862

The night was too dark for my liking. There was an array of small campfires that spread among the small field of about an acre, and it was still too dark. The sky lacked stars and a moon — most likely hidden behind the clouds that threatened to rain down on us earlier in the day. When nightfall came, not only had darkness come with it, but also an unnerving silence. The sweltering air smelled of gunpowder, sweat, fight, and fatigue — even though we were outdoors, and the stench was thick and heavy. A sporadic gun shot was heard here and there; most likely soldiers hunting for food or shooting at the rodents that roamed the field.

My back rested against the large tree behind me. I pulled my boots off my aching feet and flexed my cramped toes. Horseback or not, the trek from Shiloh was one hell of a journey. I was pretty sure I hadn't slept in days, but it felt more like weeks. Smudges of dirt streaked across my face, and I wouldn't doubt if my sandy-blond hair was just as dirty. I hadn't been able to clean up properly in weeks. The last full-night sleep I could remember having was weeks prior to marching into Shiloh; and even then, sleep was light and I was up before dawn. Exhaustion plagued me, as it did my men. We stopped to unwind before we headed towards Memphis to intersect the Confederates.

General Grant's plan was to take a hold of the Mississippi River in order to cut off the rebels' supplies that chugged up the river on a steamboat. No supplies, no victory. Considering it was Grant's idea, it was a solid plan. He hadn't steered us wrong yet; though I'm sure a majority of my company would most likely disagree with me on that thought. We were at war, and war meant death. It wasn't a hard concept to understand, but it wasn't a concept that was easy to accept either. No matter the number of battles won, there were always going to be lives lost in the end.

A loud crash of thunder shook the camp, followed by iridescent streaks of lightning across the sky. With the heat as it had been, rain seemed very welcoming for the moment. Not many of us had shelter we could take if it were to rain, not that many of us probably would. We were only a mile or so away from the river, but the rain seemed more logical to cool off in. I wedged my canteen between two rocks to keep it from falling over. If the rain did come, I'd have a full canteen of water by morning. I lifted my eyes to watch my men follow suit as they wedged their canteens between logs or whatever they could find that would keep the canteens upright. I chuckled under my breath when I watched Private Stubbs place his between his boots, then placed two large rocks inside his boots to keep them upright.

Private Matthew Stubbs was one of the youngest men in my company at only seventeen. He lied when he registered to enter the Union; stating he was nineteen at the time. With a quick glance, Stubbs looked as if he could be older than that, even with his baby face. The young man was a tall and lanky, but held his own in a fight. I commended him for that.

He wasn't educated — illiterate, even, but he knew his weaponry forwards and backwards and was a dead shot. He was the only sharpshooter in my company, and his mission was to take out Price when we reached Memphis.

The subtle silence was interrupted by Stubbs' voice, "Captain Creed?"

I looked up to see Stubbs along with three other soldiers huddled around a low fire that could be doused at any moment if the clouds decided to open and rain down on us. "What is it, Stubbs?" I called back in a low tone as I set my mud-caked boots down beside my hat and flexed my cramped toes again. I'd lost most of my uniform. There wasn't any practicality to it. What soldier needed white gloves, and a sash to kill a man? Not me. My socks were worn through with holes. The wool material looked like a potato sack that had been through hell.

My wife Leona would not have approved. The thought of her scolding me for having holes in my socks brought a faint smile to my lips.

"What time are we moving out, sir?" Stubbs asked. I glanced over at the worn soldiers who crowded around the tiny fire, watching me expectantly for my answer. Their faces were lit up by the smoldering flames, but even in the dim light I could see how tired they were, like me. Possibly more so. Their eyes seemed empty of any life, only remaining open because rest was now a luxury not a necessity.

We were all plagued with worry, wear, and pain. One would probably never guess I was thirty years old. The last time I had looked in the mirror, I saw a haggard man with a dirty beard staring back at me. Sacks of weariness hung under my eyes, and my weather-beaten skin looked like that of an older man. Twenty-five was rather old for the other gentlemen. Most of the company was about a hundred men; of my company, more than half were in their teens, including Stubbs.

"Dawn." I answered back. My voice sounded unfamiliar to me — it was deeper than normal and hoarse from the irritation in my throat. I lifted my chin, and stroked my tangled beard just as another ear-splitting crash of thunder sounded overhead. I looked over to Stubbs and the other men with a wry smirk, "Assuming, we aren't drowned by Mother Nature in the morning." The men chuckled at my dry attempt at a joke before they turned back to their campfire.

I laid my head back against the trunk of the tree. My eyes wanted to close; but they stayed open to watch the silhouette of the leaves move in the gentle wind. The lull of the movement made my eyelids heavier than they were.

The leaves were hard to see against the backdrop of the dark, cloudy sky. I squinted to make out an outline.

I took a deep, calming breath and sighed. I pictured being at home on my front porch with my darling, Leona. It had been almost a year since I'd seen her face, with the exception of the picture of her I carried. It was folded and creased from being opened and closed many times. It became my lucky charm as it stayed close to my heart inside the breast pocket of my sack coat. Never did I take it out in front of the other men. Only when I found peace by myself would I take it out and stare at it. The picture was a brassy yellow, but I could remember every detail in vivid color about her.

Her long, dark hair that hung in loose waves down her back unless she pinned it up, her vivid lilac eyes that smiled when she smiled, and the beautiful pink glow of her cheeks.

'My beautiful Leona, I promised you I would return home, and I will'.

I wasn't sure what day it was, but I was sure it had been a few weeks since I'd gotten a letter sent out to Leona. Since we were heading to meet with a regiment in Memphis, I pondered writing her a letter and having it sent to her when we reached our destination. At least she'd know I was still alive, and that I was okay — this woman was prone to wearing a pacing hole through the kitchen floor when she was worried.

The thoughts of my wife were interrupted by lightning that lit up the sky again after a low rumble of thunder in the distance, followed by an eerie howl.

It wasn't a series of howls, like a pack of wolves; but one, single howl and it wasn't any normal wolf bay. My men heard it as well — each straightening up and turning towards the forest behind me. I hurriedly shoved my feet back into my boots, forgetting about my hat, and pushed myself off the ground. The rumbling and various thuds in the forest were heard not only by me, but by those closest to me. My heart began to beat heavily in my chest. A drop of sweat rolled down my forehead, along the bridge of my nose, then dropped off. My muscles were tensed as if I were ready to go into battle.

Another ungodly howl followed, but this time it was closer. I heard my men scramble to their feet and gather behind me to watch for whatever was charging in our direction. They readied their arms as I pulled my pistol from its holster. My eyes glanced down for only a second at my sword that sat propped up against the tree. I lifted my blue eyes and squinted into the darkness. I stared as far as my eyes would allow into the woods, trying to focus into the pitch black for whatever was approaching us; and approaching us fast.

"Cap, what is it?" I heard Private Pettit ask from behind me in a whisper, "Is it a wolf?"

If it were a wolf, it wasn't like any wolf I heard before, "It's something," I said in a hushed tone, never taking my eyes off the blackness.

Then silence.

No moving brush, no huffing…Nothing. The silence lasted far too long, and whatever it was, it was watching us.

Goosebumps raised along my forearms. I forced down a shiver when I saw a pair of glowing yellow eyes staring back at us from inside the forest.

Another howl ripped from the darkness, followed by a vicious snarl. Startled, I stumbled a step back, before aiming my trembling pistol into the blinding darkness, but the eyes had disappeared.

There was not enough time for me to even make sense of what was happening nor to defend myself. Within seconds, a large black mass launched out of the woods and tackled me, hard enough that I landed on top of the smoldering wood that was once the soldiers' fire.

My pistol dropped from my hand as I shoved at its shoulders to keep its snapping fangs away from my face. I struggled with all my strength against the large beast, but it was useless. The thing had overpowered and pinned me to the ground. Beneath me the embers burned through my coat, searing my skin.

In the midst of the attack, I heard the chaos ensuing around me of men yelling and running. Orders were shouted, but I couldn't make sense of any of it for the moment. I was avoiding getting torn to shreds.

My legs were pinned underneath the heavy beast, but I struggled and managed to land a harsh kick to its knee joint, causing it to yelp before it raised a black-clawed "hand" and struck me. Its claws ripped through my jacket and my shirt, right into the flesh of my left shoulder.

It bent its fingers, tearing and severing the muscles, ligaments, and tendons in my shoulder. I felt the tips of its claws score across my bone as it continued to drag them through my arm.

I yelled in excruciating pain. My head fell back, and my left arm went limp, and for a moment I believed it was going to rip my arm off.

The beast froze, its fingers still embedded in my shoulder. Those glowing yellow eyes narrowed as my assailant slowly turned its head to look over its shoulder. Private Stubbs stood behind the monster, his face twisted in fear. A bayonet jutted out of the beast's back between the shoulder blades; but the blade didn't seem to hurt the creature in the least.

The assault only seemed to piss the beast off more.

I panted, cringed, then tried to force myself to speak; but all I could do was grit my teeth and grimace as his claws scraped along the sinew that held my arm to the rest of my body.

"Run!" I shouted out in a strain to Stubbs.

Stubbs didn't follow my command — he only took a few clumsy steps backwards away from the beast. It snarled as saliva dripped from its long canines and oozed onto my cheek. The viscous drool rolled down into my ear.

The thing pushed up off of me, withdrawing its razor-sharp claws from my shoulder and about-faced Stubbs.

I rolled onto my right side, holding my shoulder as I winced in pain. Blood gushed between my fingers, pooling beneath me and creating a mess of bloody mud. My other men scrambled to get me to my feet. They grabbed me by my jacket and hoisted my large frame to my feet. My knees felt weak, I was losing a profuse amount of blood, and I was dizzy.

I staggered but remained on my feet as I watched the beast lurch towards Stubbs. It was as if everyone was afraid to move, our feet cemented to the dusty ground beneath our boots.

I will never forget Stubbs' expression was of sheer terror. His brown eyes were wide with fear, his mouth agape as he craned his head back to look up at the enormous beast that towered over him.

It had to be at least seven feet tall on its hind legs. That's impossible… Wolves didn't get that big, did they? It not only stood on its hind legs, but it resembled the stature of a man. Even in the face of danger, I could remember every single detail of what the beast looked like. Five fingers, each tipped with black, dagger-like claws, dark fur that covered its entire body, a tail, the ears and muzzle resembled that of a wolf, but it wasn't just a wolf, it was a demon of some sort.

The creature had taken one last step forward, standing only inches away from the Private. "Stubbs!" I hollered to my soldier. The beast turned its immense torso to sneer at me, then turned its attention back to Stubbs.

The bayonet still jutted out of its back, but it seemed Stubbs was now its target. Stubbs' eyes never left the beast; they remained wide, and the Private trembled where he stood. Within half a breath, the beast lifted its monstrous arm and swung; its claws severed Stubbs' head clean off of his body.

Everyone yelled in horror as we watched Stubbs' body fall, and his head rolled back into the dark forest. The others scattered away from the horrific scene — escaping for their lives.

I could only stand there and watch, my limbs wouldn't move. I couldn't even feel the pain anymore. My entire body felt like it was weighed down by lead.

Stray tears, blood, and sweat cascaded down my cheeks.

It took everything I had left in me to finally move. I turned and grabbed the sword from a lieutenant's sheath. The shearing sound it made as I removed it caused the beast to whip back around towards me and my company. It's dark brow-line narrowed in a menace, arms outstretched, fingers spread. It puffed out its chest, lifted its chin, and released an ear-piercing, inhuman howl that made my blood curdle.

Its eyes landed back on me. I could see in its glare, it wanted to finish what it had started. The wolf lowered down onto all fours and crept towards us. I stumbled backwards, yanking myself from their grasp. My legs shook, my breath quivered in fear as I knew, I knew this thing was going to kill me. Kill us.

A deep, fierce growl sounded from the beast as it crept closer, and then it lunged at me. I knocked back the men that were beside me and lifted my sword with my uninjured hand. With a pained grunt, I swung it at the airborne beast, decapitating it before it could reach me.

The large, fur-covered body fell flat onto the ground, a huff of dust surrounding its torso, and the head rolled toward another soldier's feet.

The soldier scurried backwards and tripped over a log as he stared in panic at the head. Its eyes were still open, the brightness of the yellow dulling. The mouth remained in a permanent, vicious sneer.

I dropped the sword and fell to my knees as the excruciating pain returned. My mind went blank, no thoughts, no questions, just pain. Complete agony ripped through me like nothing I had ever felt before.

"Let's get him to the infirmary tent. He's losing blood." I heard Lieutenant Dickens — my right hand, call out to the men in a rush. It was blurred, but I remembered being hoisted from my feet and dragged across the field. My head fell back as I cried out though I was being tortured.

I'd endured my fair share of pain, but nothing could compare to what I felt. My shoulder and each deep wound felt as if they were on fire. Never mind the burns I received on my back when I fell into the fire. This was something entirely worse.

I'd seen grown men cry, but I had never done it myself until this moment.

The pain spread quickly from my shoulder into the remaining muscles and bones of my body. My screams echoed throughout the field where my company remained. I struggled to hold onto my vision, but it was quickly becoming clouded and dark as I pled internally — 'Just let me die, God, please, just let me die now' — but death would not come to me. Not soon enough.

"What the hell was that thing?!" I heard the words from what seemed like from a distance, but it was one of the soldiers assisting in my being moved.

"No earthly idea, but it's dead. We'll worry about it after we get the Cap taken care of," Dickens answered back in a haste.

They dragged me inside the small infirmary tent. I was handed off to our medic, Sergeant Dove and laid on a cot.

They cut off my blood-soaked jacket and shirt. My fingers curled into tight fists, I gnashed my teeth as I convulsed on the bed with solid desire to die.

Whatever was coursing through me was burning from the inside out.

"What in the…?" Sergeant Dove said as every man in the tent took a step back from the cot. Time stopped and the tent grew silent with the exception of my shouting and heavy breaths.

"Dear God…" Lieutenant Dickens trailed off in surprise; and that was the last thing I heard before the darkness won.

Cassy Crownover

Cassy Crownover is a horror enthusiast, writer of several genres, comedian, and a freelance graphic designer from Tampa, Florida.

The Doctor and The Lady

By Delia Remington

Flames flickered in Mary's eyes as she tore another page from the journal she had stolen from Doctor Polidori's room in the Villa Diodati. Frowning, she crumpled the paper in her hand, then tossed it in among the flames. With crackles and hisses, the paper shriveled and curled in upon itself as the fire licked away the words, leaving black traces that spread across the surface, merging with the scrawled letters, before disintegrating with startling finality. Smoke carried away the words, and she watched them disappear with satisfaction and relief. Her face showed no remorse.

She had been smart enough not to make detailed notes about the events of the summer in her own journal. Still, she had naively believed that what she was learning from that man would be good research for the story she was writing. After all, John Polidori was a doctor newly graduated from the University of Edinburgh. He had been a prodigy. He was well-versed on the latest medical techniques. Who better to explain the newest research on the effects of electricity on animal tissues than a man who had witnessed a demonstration of Galvani's experiment. Moreover, he understood her passion for writing and had begun his own horror story about a vampyre. He had been happy to assist her.

Her husband, Percy Shelley, had been fascinated by Mary's story idea. It was in his nature. He had a fierce curiosity with no thought of consequences. When she'd explained her dream that morning after their writing contest was announced, he had suggested that she talk with the doctor and expand her knowledge on the subject. It had seemed like good advice.

The young doctor, initially hired as physician to Lord Byron, who had seemed so friendly that she called him her "little brother" had turned out to be a spy and a monster in their midst. She had trusted him. Confided her secrets. He had betrayed her utterly.

* * *

Glancing out the window, I could see Mrs. Shelley, for so she called herself, walking across the lawn. Her face was flushed with exertion, and for a moment the clouds parted to let in a shaft of sunlight that shone on her hair. Her dress had a great deal of décolletage, and even from my distant vantage I could see her heaving bosom, her pale skin shown to great advantage. Searching the facade of the house, she saw me standing there and met my gaze with an expression that showed she was conscious of the effect of her beauty. She lifted her skirts as she began to climb the steps, exposing her ankles in the process. I licked my lips and tore my eyes away, moving from the window to go downstairs to meet her.

"My dear Doctor," she said, her voice a little breathless. "I hope you will not think me impertinent for coming to see you unannounced."

"Of course not." I bowed and found my eyes again drawn to her breasts. I swallowed hard and took her hand, kissing it lightly. "Such friends as we are have no need of formal invitations. Do come in."

She laughed, stepping a little closer. "Thank you."

Her nearness made me blush, and I cleared my throat to cover my embarrassment. "Have you come on a medical matter?"

"Yes," she said. "I require your knowledge and expertise."

"Shall we go into my study to sit and talk a while, madam?" I took a half step away, turning to gesture down the hall.

Removing her hat and her wrap, she nodded. "That would be very nice. Thank you."

We walked down the hall together. I felt her presence beside me in the same way a blind man can sense the direction of the sun from its warmth radiating on his skin. It was all I could do to resist touching her. "She is married. She is married," I kept repeating in my mind, but the knowledge that this was not technically true kept interrupting my thought.

I knew that her sister, Claire Clairmont, had been carrying on an affair with Lord Byron. It had been going on for months. She made a halfhearted attempt at discretion while in public, but when thrown together in close quarters as we were, she dropped all pretense. As for milord, clearly he found Miss Clairmont diverting, but not worthy of his deeper affections. Though no one had as yet spoken openly about it, I saw all the signs of pregnancy in Claire.

Walking into the surgery, I thus expected Mrs. Shelley to request that I examine her sister or perhaps even attempt an abortion. With each step, I rehearsed my response. The objections were at the ready by the time we sat down together.

Byron had given over an entire room in the house to my work, and the walls were lined with shelves full of little glass jars, drawers full of instruments, and the latest technological advances including a microscope and surgical tools. He had even indulged my whims by purchasing a Voltaic pile for generating electricity. My pet area of study was somnambulism, and I intended to use electro shock treatments in an attempt to discover its effects on subjects who suffered from sleepwalking. Mr. Shelley, himself, had volunteered to take part in my experiments, but I had not yet completed my preparations for the research.

Imagine my surprise, therefore, when Mrs. Shelley began to speak and I discovered that her intentions were to do with neither of these possibilities.

I crossed one leg over the other, folding my hands on my knee, and regarded her. "How can I help you, my dear Mrs. Shelley?"

"Please, call me Mary," she said, her lips curling into a soft smile.

This little intimacy made me relax a little, and I unclasped my hands and bowed my head slightly. "As you wish. You may call me John."

She took a deep breath, and I waited, trying to give her the space to gather her courage to talk of indelicate matters.

"You know that I am writing a story for our little contest, do you not?"

Her question, having no clear relevance to the topics I had been anticipating, took me aback. Nodding slowly, I tried my best to keep my confusion from showing on my face. "Erm, yes. That is to say, I recall your discussion of your nightmare. The one about the creature."

"That's the one. I wondered if you could help me gain some rudimentary medical knowledge that would help me expand that idea into a longer tale." Seeing my confusion, she leaned forward, blushing slightly. "Please don't misunderstand me. I have no aspiration to become a physician, and I do not want to take up too much of your valuable time. I simply hope to learn enough that I can speak of these matters in very broad terms and not seem ridiculous."

I sat back with pleased astonishment. "You flatter me, dear lady."

"Not at all. You are recently graduated from the University of Edinburgh, are you not?"

Smiling back at her, I nodded. "Indeed."

"Then you will be well-versed in all of the newest techniques and theories."

I nodded again, unsure where this was going. "Yes, but I fail to see..."

"What I want to know is, doctor, is it possible? Or rather, if science continues to advance in the pursuit of medicine, would it be possible to bring the dead back to life?"

I blinked with surprise. "I...I don't know. We are not there now, not yet, certainly. But who knows what wonders the future might hold. Perhaps we will find the secret to everlasting life one day. Yes, I suppose one day it might be possible. But..."

She leaned forward and patted my knee. "I knew you would know. I have heard of Signore Galvoni and his experiments with electricity on the legs of dead frogs. And when I was a child in London, a gentleman tried to reanimate the body of a man who had been hung. Father described it to me. He said the man purchased the corpse from the jailer an hour after the public execution, brought the body to a medical theatre, and proceeded to use electrical shocks on it. Though the dead man did not return to life, he did sit up, and open his eyes upon the crowd, and more than one doctor observing the procedure was shocked to see it reanimate, just as Galvoni's frog legs had done."

Without thinking, I crossed myself, but her description filled my mind with both revulsion and curiosity.

Embarrassed by my reaction to her enthusiasm, she bit her lip. "I hope I haven't shocked you, John."

I cleared my throat. "No, of course not. I have read of such experiments. They were the subject of fierce debate during my studies."

Her face brightened again. "I thought so. So...do you think you could help me?"

"I don't understand what you mean. Help in what way? What exactly do you want to know?"

"Well, can you help me answer my basic question? Is such a thing possible?"

"I'm afraid I still don't know how you wish me to proceed."

"Let me speak plainly, then. I wish to observe you conducting an experiment of that nature."

My jaw dropped, and I stood up abruptly. "What you ask is illegal, madam. Conducting autopsies is a criminal offense in Switzerland. I could be arrested and hanged."

"Only if we are caught. And anyway, I would help. And Byron is wealthy and powerful. He would make certain you were never convicted of such a crime. But think of the possibilities! You would be famous! The savior of mankind. The doctor who found the key to immortality. Just think of it."

Her eyes pleaded for understanding, watching me as I paced the room to keep up with the speed of my thoughts. "Do you know what you are suggesting, Mary? It goes against nature. Or at least the law will see it that way."

"But you and I, are we not above such superstition? You are a man of science. Doesn't your curiosity compel you to search for the answers? Have you ever lost someone you cared about, John? What if you could bring that person back to life? Hold that human being in your arms once more and never have to suffer such pain and loss again. Isn't that worth the danger?"

She rose and crossed the room to touch my arm. Her eyes were wet as I turned to look at her, and I could not help but be compelled by her plea. "John, I am a mother. William is a beautiful child, full of life and joy. But I had another child who died not long after her birth. Her life was cut painfully short. I would give anything to have her alive again and reaching her potential. What mother would not do the same? Each time I look at William, I feel both happiness and fear of loss. If anything should happen to him, I could not bear it. But you could ensure that mothers would never have to experience that sorrow."

My heart ached at the tragedy of her loss, and I was moved to take her hand in my own. "What you want isn't possible."

"Not yet," she said.

"You don't know what you're asking. You want me to play God."

Mary laughed. "My husband says there is no god."

"He's an atheist, then?"

She nodded. "But whether God exists or not, surely he would wish us to help reduce the suffering in the world."

I pulled away and began pacing again, looking down at the floor while my mind raced.

"Let me ask you this, doctor. Would such an experiment cause pain to the person who is already dead?"

"No, but..."

"And if it causes that person no true harm, then it is only scientific ignorance that is the basis for such laws."

I sighed. "True, but..."

"Then you admit that you see no true impediment." She smiled at me triumphantly. "Please, then, doctor. Help me. While you are saving humanity from death itself, I will write a story that proves the benefit of such research. No one afterward could help but understand and applaud your efforts."

Her mind was quick and fixed in it's resolve. I frowned, unable to think of a way to refuse her what she wanted. In fact, seeing the earnest fervor in her eyes, I was certain that if I gave her an outright "no" as an answer, she might try to accomplish the thing on her own and get herself in trouble if left to her own devices. She was naive and used to getting her way, and the combination was alarming given the situation. She fully believed in this scheme of hers, and she would not be dissuaded.

Therefore, despite my own certainty that her plan was not feasible and my fears of discovery by police, I resolved to do exactly as she asked in order to protect her from any such foolhardy attempts. I hoped that participating in her experiment would put an end to her macabre interest.

* * *

From the bottom of a rectangular hole, I made a muffled grunt as dirt flew upwards in an arch. Mary held the lamp gingerly, shielding the flame from prying eyes with her windswept cape.

"John? Is it long now?" She looked around furtively. "What if someone comes?"

I looked up, my shirtsleeves rolled to the elbow, dirt smudging my high cheekbones. Her eyes glittered in the moonlight. "We are very nearly there, I am sure. If you see anyone coming, leave the lantern and hide yourself. I will take whatever consequences upon myself. You needn't fear."

I was filled with guilt. I was doing this at her request, and if we were caught we could face serious charges. The fear of incarceration fell upon me, and I suddenly realized just what it would mean for her son if she were taken to jail. "What were we thinking? Mary, perhaps we should leave. It's not worth it."

But I heaved my shovel one last time and hit something solid, the sound reverberating amongst the gravestones with a resounding thunk. I froze at the noise. "I found it. Just a few moments, and we will have what we came for."

I dug until I had uncovered the top of the coffin. The wood creaked with my weight. It was a plain pine box, and I was filled with terror at the idea I might step onto a sudden weak spot and find my foot crashing through onto the corpse inside. And yet, that corpse was what the thing we had come for, wasn't it?

No point in squeamishness now. We had come this far. There was no turning back after this.

"I have it," I said, my voice rising from the depths of the grave." Hand me the crowbar, if you would, please, madam."

And there it was in horrible juxtaposition. My polite deference to her and at the same time the dreadful purpose of our endeavor. But I was at the point of no return. The bile rose in my throat. Panic made my skin prickle, and I ached for us to run. Instead,

I took a deep breath, put my hand out for the crowbar as she handed it down into the gaping hole.

The coffin thudded and creaked as the nails came loose one by one. I held my breath until my lungs began to burn. At last, there was one loud cracking sound that made my heart go to my throat, and my pulse pounded in my ears. "I'm in."

She gulped audibly and bent down to whisper. "What now?"

"I will hand you up the body. Thank goodness he hasn't been here more than a day."

"You'll hand me...doctor, maybe this really is a bad idea."

"He's wrapped in a winding sheet. You won't have to touch him directly."

Before she had time to say anything more, I pushed the wrapped body up toward her. She put out her trembling hands and took hold of the body. The corpse was cold through the fabric. I grunted with effort. The full weight of the body fell on top of me, and the stink of the grave overwhelmed my senses. The winding sheet suffocated me, and the corpse pinned me down, helpless, squashing the breath from me. I thought I might faint for the first time in my life, and the panic made me shove helplessly to escape from under the gruesome thing pressing all too real on top of me. I bit my lip to hold back from crying out. Just as I felt my vision swim, the weight rolled away, and I took deep gulps of precious air once more. I clambered out of the grave to find her on the ground beneath the body. She had fallen back into the dirt, struggling with her ungainly petticoats. I rolled the corpse to one side, then stood next to her, holding out my hand to help her up. "I am so sorry, madam. Are you hurt?"

She took my hand and stood, shaking her head over and over, unable to formulate a reply. I brushed dirt from her skirts and looked up at her, feeling boyish and shy. The absurdity of the gesture, so in contrast with the events of the night, made me laugh in spite of everything. She looked taken aback by this reaction, stepping away from me as though I had struck her.

"We need to get the body on the cart." I put on an air of business, and I could tell she was angry, though whether at herself or at me, I couldn't tell.

Somehow, when we had discussed our plans, I had not envisioned the two of us actually hoisting a body into a wooden cart. I hadn't thought through the practicalities of the job. She was not really strong enough for the task. And so I found myself taking the bulk of the weight, hefting it by the torso, the body's head resting on my shoulder. Mary held the feet and did her best to keep quiet. I heard the winding sheet tear as we struggled to lift our heavy burden. By the time we managed to maneuver it into place, we were both winded. Dead weight, indeed. I then began the laborious task of shoveling the dirt back into the open grave. I longed to be gone, but there was less chance of our activities being discovered if there was no gaping hole that made our crime obvious.

At last, the job was done, and though the dirt did not pile as high on the top as it had before, still it did disguise our presence much better than I had expected.

"Aren't you going to tamp it down?" she said.

I shook my head. "I'm afraid my shoes with their English marks on the sole might give me away."

"Oh," she said. "Of course."

"Let's away before the caretaker rouses from his slumber." I pointed toward the clock in the church tower. "It is only two hours till dawn, and while we have been lucky up to this point, I do not wish to test it further."

I brushed the dirt from my hands, and then we covered the body with a heavy tarpaulin. We strapped it down with ropes on all sides, and then began the slow trudge back up the mountain to the Villa Diodati.

Never have I walked so far, at least so it seemed that night. I strained to pull the cart behind myself while Mary pushed from the rear when the wheels stuck on the uneven cobblestones. The fog turned to a mizzling rain, so that by the time we reached our destination, we were soaked to the bone and half frozen.

I pulled the cart around toward the back and stopped by the kitchen door. The servants would still be abed, I thought, and this entry was nearer to my surgery. Though I longed for help to carry the body inside, I knew that Mary would be of no use in this capacity. "Get the doors for me, if you would, please," I said to her, hoisting the body over one shoulder like an enormous sack of ungainly potatoes. One arm had come loose from the winding sheet and flopped to the ground, fingers just touching the back of my calves as I walked.

The pressure of my shoulder into the stomach cavity of the corpse made it begin to fart as the gases within were forced out. I gagged at the foul stench, but there was nothing for it.

The head of the corpse banged against the door as I walked through, and I found myself whispering, "I'm sorry," even though I knew it was ridiculous. Until that moment, it had seemed just a nameless body, a thing, but here I was, acknowledging its personhood.

No good going down that road. A doctor must be objective. The body was a thing. A wonder of scientific curiosity. Nothing more. The soul which had animated it had fled, and all we were left with was an empty husk. Like a snake which had shed its skin, the corpse was left behind after the soul had moved on.

I told myself these things as I struggled toward my surgery room, trying to keep my mind from being overwhelmed with guilt and horror at what we were doing.

* * *

With a great deal of effort, we placed the body on the examination table. I cut the winding sheet from toe to head, letting the fabric drape to either side. The room filled with the scent of rotting flesh.

Mary stared, standing stock still with fear. "Is that normal? The black around his mouth and eyes, I mean. And his fingernails are black too."

"Yes," I said. "The blood has pooled in those areas like a bruise."

"I see."

Reaching into my pocket, I pulled out the key to my room and crossed the room to lock the door. She gave me a look of alarm. "We don't want to be disturbed while we complete our work."

Though I spoke matter-of-factly, I was far from calm inside. I had already played out several scenarios in which our crime was discovered, and I could not get those ideas out of my mind.

Frightened though I was, I managed to get my face under control so that when I turned back around to face her, my emotions did not show.

I removed my dirty jacket and waistcoat, tossing them to the side, and then rolled up my sleeves to begin the practical matter of work we had in store.

"You...you're starting now?" Her voice trembled slightly, and I looked back to see her still gaping at the body.

"The sooner we begin, the sooner we finish and can hide the evidence." I walked over to the washstand and scrubbed my hands and arms ferociously, trying to remove the grime from beneath my fingernails.

Ablutions completed, I moved to gather my surgical implements from the cabinet.

"What are those for?"

I pulled out each of the tools in succession, naming them all one by one as I arrayed them on the table. Amputation saws and knives. Gorget. Bullet probe. Silkworm Ligatures. Tweezers. Forceps. Trephine. Skull Saw.

Pausing, I looked up at Mary who was still standing like a statue. "Are you going to make any notes as I work?"

"Oh. Oh yes." She reached into the pocket of her coat and brought out a small notebook and a pencil. I could tell she was grateful to have a job to occupy her mind and keep her from the overwhelming realization of what we were doing. "Could you go over that one more time, please?"

I repeated myself once more. Then I began the autopsy on the body in earnest, dictating my findings as I went.

The deceased was a male, aged around forty five, with a balding head and stature over six feet. He wore a threadbare suit which was clearly his best. His hands were rough and callused, indicating to me that he had worked doing manual labor for his entire adult life.

Very carefully, I opened the man's jacket and shirt front, revealing his torso to the waist. That done, I could see the cause of death easily. He had been shot in the chest and had been dead for no more than a day or two. His belly was beginning to look distended, his eyes and tongue bulged slightly, and his skin was gray and cold to touch.

Mary's pencil scratched across the paper furiously as she wrote down every detail of my observations. From the corner of my eye, I could see that some of her hair had escaped the pins that held it back into a bun, and she had tucked it behind her ear to get it out of her face. She had a look of clinical observation, all emotion drained from her face. It chilled me to the bone to see it on such an otherwise beautiful countenance.

I cleared my throat, returning to the work at hand. "I'm going to remove the bullet in his chest and then suture the wound closed."

She looked up with a puzzled expression as if to ask me why I would do such a thing.

"If we want to raise this body back to life, the wound will have to be repaired."

"Wait. Doctor, what about the man's blood?"

It was my turn to look back at her in confusion. "What about it?"

"Well, if he's lost a lot of blood, how could he live after this?"

"My dear lady, I have no illusions that we will be able to bring this man back to life. His gun shot wound was fatal. The best we can hope for this long after death is a few moments of animation. His consciousness is gone. All that we have left is the husk of his body without a soul."

Her forehead furrowed in frustration. "But then we have failed already. It has been a waste."

I shook my head. "No. If we can demonstrate that the body can be reanimated, even in this state, then we can prove that it might be possible, using electrical impulses, to bring a person without such extensive injury back to life, provided the shock is given quickly enough.

Disappointment filled her eyes. "So we needed a fresher corpse, you mean. And someone who died of natural causes rather than trauma."

"Yes. But for the purposes of what you proposed, our experiment will still yield valuable information. The road to scientific discovery is a long one, dear lady, and there are many steps toward the goal. I know of no medical or scientific principle which was proven with one experiment alone. Progress is made in increments, and the true natural philosopher must be patient enough to prove the accuracy of his theories over the course of several attempts. What we are attempting tonight is only the first step."

Biting her lip, she listened thoughtfully, then looked away over her shoulder toward the window nearby. Dawn was just breaking, and the cold gray light was beginning to filter through the curtains. She peered out for a few moments with a long contemplative stare, then she walked decisively over to the window and pulled the curtains closed.

"We do not want to risk discovery. Let's get on with it, then, doctor."

I labored for the better part of half an hour to remove the bullet that had lodged itself in the man's left lung. It had missed striking his heart by inches. A couple of his ribs were cracked, and I had to break them with my extractor in order to take out the bullet. It finally came loose with a little pop, and putrefying liquid oozed from the wound.

Gathering my needle and silkworm ligatures, I closed the wound, though without blood to adhere the flesh together, there were puckered gaps between the stitches that could not be fixed. Still, it was the best I could do under the circumstances.

"Now what?" she said, her voice in a cracked whisper. I could see the dark circles of exhaustion under her eyes. We had been up all night long at our ghastly work. But we had come this far, and we had to continue until we finished what we had begun.

"Now," I said, "we administer electricity and see what happens."

I heard her breath hiss as she gasped through her clenched teeth. Ignoring this, I walked with a steadiness I did not feel over to the Voltaic pile. I had only used the battery to generate long arching sparks for a parlor trick. Never had I imagined putting it to this sort of use.

Two hand sheathed coils of wire were attached to the apparatus, and each end was fitted with a wooden handle through which cylindrical rod of copper had been threaded. These copper rods extended out past the wooden handles, terminating in flat disks which could be used to shock an object. Grimly, I picked up the machine and turned to face the corpse, setting my jaw with a firm resolve.

I placed the Voltaic pile on the table near the body. Taking a deep breath, I took up the wooden handles and touched them both to the sides of our subject's arm experimentally. The fingers jerked, and the muscles spasmed as the sparks did their work. Small scorch marks appeared on the skin, and we could smell burned flesh. Mary dropped her pencil. I heard it roll across the floor, but she did not bend to pick it up.

Pulling back, I looked at the body with a critical eye. The small test of the equipment made me bold, and I wondered if next I could start the heart beating once again. I gathered my courage, stepped forward again, and touched both disks to the sternum.

The entire body bucked on the table this time, and more of the putrid gas and fluid was expelled. Mary turned her head and wretched into a nearby basin. I stepped back, covering my nose and mouth against the stench.

"Oh god," she said. "I can't bear it. Stop. Please stop."

Yet, though I was horrified by the experiment, I was determined to complete the last of my attempts at reanimation. "Once more, and then I will be satisfied."

Gathering my courage, I brought the disks firmly against both sides of the man's skull. His eyes and mouth opened, the face contorting into a grimace. The bloated tongue waggled from his blackened lips, and a bit of putrid fluid leaked from the corner of his mouth. But it was the eyes that were worst of all. Seeing that dead man sightlessly staring up at the ceiling was the single most devastating and horrifying experience of my life, and the memory of it will haunt me till the end of my days. They looked out with an expression of hopeless emptiness that filled me with a mortal dread because in that moment I realized that all of us one day would have that same vacant stare. Even me.

I backed away and let go of the handles of the device. "Enough."

"Oh doctor, what are we going to do with this wretched thing?" She couldn't bring herself to look at the body. Instead her gaze stayed fixed on the floor.

"We are going to bury him."

Her voice rose to near hysteria, and she shrank back against the wall, trembling. "I can't. I can't...touch that thing again."

I turned to face her, snapping with sudden rage and sorrow and shame. "This was your idea. Every moment of this was your mind's creation. We will bury this man, and you will help me. You have a responsibility here. Do you understand me, Mary?"

Cringing, she shook her head over and over. "I can't. I can't."

She kept repeating it, and I realized that she was in shock. With two strides, I was in front of her, and I slapped her hard across the face. "You will."

The look of stunned surprise on her face made me step back. She was just a girl. Only 19 years old. And I was not much older. I felt suddenly very young and foolish. "I'm sorry for that. I had to do something to bring you back to your senses. Forgive me."

"You're a monster." Her words were barely a whisper, but they cut deeper than any surgeon's tool. It was more than just the slap that she blamed me for. I saw her eyes slide over toward the body, and I knew she was talking about the entire night's work.

"I did this for you," I said. "It was all for you. I'd have done anything to make you happy. You said this was what you wanted."

She gasped. "I never wanted...this."

"We have to bury him," I said simply, despair welling up in my soul. "Before we are found out."

It took her a moment to reply, and I could almost see her mind working as she thought through the situation. "We can't take him back. I can't go back to that place."

"No," I said. "It's too late for that. He will have to be buried here."

"On the grounds? But the servants..."

"In the cellar."

And so that is what we did. Though she hated me, she helped me. Though it was wretched work, we brought him down into the bottom of that house and buried him beneath the floor.

We never spoke of the events of that night from that day forward.

* * *

"Doctor Polidori," said John Murray, leaning forward to frown under fierce eyebrows, "I cannot possibly pay you the rest of the money we discussed in our original agreement. You have not delivered your end of our bargain. I paid you an advance of £500 for your memoirs of your journey in the employ of Lord Byron, with an additional £500 to be paid upon delivery and review for publication. Instead, you hand me a nearly illegible journal with an entire month's worth of entries torn out. Moreover, you were dismissed by the man himself and were unable to complete the journey which you were paid to describe."

He tossed the journal across his desk toward me, and I caught it before it fell to the floor. "I can explain."

With a dismissive wave of his hand, Mr. Murray cut me off. "Let me be frank. I am a publisher. My business is producing and selling books. I cannot sell this, sir. There is no book which can be produced from that notebook. Our contract is at an end."

"But sir, if you will only…"

"Good day, sir." He rose from his desk and crossed to the door, holding it open for me.

Defeated and heartbroken, I fought back tears, but somehow I put on my hat and managed to walk out of that room on my own power. The noise of the press was overpowering, and the scent of the ink and paper made a heady perfume that permeated the publishing house.

I was in disgrace, and there was nothing I could do about it. Without my job and reputation as a physician, I had hoped that I might at least find a modicum of success as an author, and yet here I was, failing even at something which had seemed to me a sure bet.

Utterly wretched, I walked out of 32 Fleet Street into the misty afternoon. There was very little money left in my pocket, and I paused to turn up the collar of my coat before heading toward St. Paul's Cathedral. I kept my eyes on the sidewalk, distracted and ashamed.

Young boys were hawking newspapers on the street, shouting out the headlines. Their faces were streaked with ink smudges, and the papers were tucked under their insufficient coats in order to keep them out of the damp. One such young man caught the sleeve of my coat as I attempted to pass. I was prepared to refuse him, but when I saw his gaunt cheeks and hungry look of desperation, I was moved by pity, and handed him a few pennies in exchange for the newspaper I did not need and could not truly afford.

Opening up the paper, I used it as shelter from the drizzle. Near the cathedral was a public house, and I went inside to warm myself and get out of the rain. I bought a pint of ale and sat down at one of the tables alone, trying to gather my courage to write a letter to my father, asking him for more money. While I sat, I decided to defer these thoughts by reading a few of the stories in my soggy paper.

Upon closer inspection, however, I discovered that what I had purchased was not actually a newspaper at all. It was Blackwood's Edinburgh Magazine, a literary review publication. There in the list of contents, was a review headline which caught my eye. It was a review of "Frankenstein, or the Modern Prometheus" by an author named Walter Scott. I stared for a moment at the title. I recognized it right away, for the name is unusual enough to be immediately memorable. It was Mary's main character's name. The one from the story she had been writing three years before. Clearly, she had used a pen name, believing that men would not respect a book written by a woman. So she had finished it at last.

I took a deep breath, feeling a momentary pang of jealousy that her book had been published but mine had not. However, curiosity got the better of me, and I turned to see what the reviewer had to say.

It was not the review itself which struck me. Instead, as I read the synopsis of the book, I was struck with a horrible sense of recognition. There in the pages of her book, she had written about the events of that awful night. And I realized with a shock that she had modeled her main character after me. Worst of all, that character was painted as a villain, hunted to the ends of the earth for his crimes against nature.

I crumpled the paper in my hand.

"You all right, then, love?" said the barmaid, passing with a tray of empty glasses. "You looks a bit queer, you do."

"I'm fine, thank you." Waving her off, I looked away, throwing the paper across the table.

In truth, I was anything but that. I would never be fine again.

Delia Remington

Delia Remington lives in an old house in a small town near the Missouri River with her Scottish terrier, Layla, and she spends her days surrounded by books and good friends.

The first novel in her **Blood Royal Saga** vampire series, *In The Blood*, won the **2018 Silver Stake Award** at the International Vampire Film and Arts Festival in Sighișoara, Romania and was a **finalist for the 2018 Midwest Book Awards** held by the Midwest Independent Publishing Association.

For more information about Delia and her writing and to subscribe to her newsletter, visit DeliaRemington.com.

The Lady In White

By Karolyne Cronin

Chapter 1: The Introduction

"Monsters are real, and ghosts are real too.
They live inside us, and sometimes, they win."
~Stephen King

We have all heard of the story. In every town, there is at least one version of this tale. There is always a lady in white that walks a highway. No one knows how she started walking her path, but someone always knows someone that has given her a ride. Usually, it is some distant cousin that they haven't seen since the last family reunion seven years before.

Her identity is uncertain, but she tends to be thought of as Mary. One would think that would deter anyone from giving their daughter that name. There are guesses as to what happened to her, but no one knows. What is certain is that her end wasn't pretty, and she will bring dread and horror to all that meet her. The most famous examples are Resurrection Mary and La Llorona.

Knowing these things, what if you were a lady in white? That you did not have a pretty ending. Not sure that what you know of yourself is actually true. Walking a path that never ends. Wishing to finally reach your destination and dreading it at the same time. Understanding deep down that you'll never find peace.

I am a lady in white. I do not know how I came to this situation. I cannot even remember who I am at times. I just feel this longing that gnaws at me. Pressing against my chest that really isn't there. Time bends, not at my will, but at the will of one not known. There are moments that seem like seconds and turn out to be years. Then there are years that last only a blink of an eye.

It is a lonely existence and one that I know will not end unless I do something. I may not be sure who I am, but I will not wander for eternity. I will make sure that I find out about my ending. I know that it will not be pretty. How could it? I am a specter of legend. From what I can remember, legends rarely ever end prettily. Still, I will figure out how to break this cycle and find a new path. There must be a way.

Chapter 2: The Legend

"Do you have an answer for me, Miss Thorpe?"

Karyna looked up at the professor with a startled look on her face. Of course, Professor Maxwell would call on her when she wasn't prepared. It was like the man knew when his students slacked off. In her defense, she hadn't slacked off per se. More than her time management skills needed improvement. She had meant to read the chapter on the traditional roles of women in myths, but it didn't happen. Instead, she got sucked into some strange article about Slenderman. Before she knew it, she looked up and it was past midnight and she was somehow was reading about vortexes. It seemed she had been caught up in another so-called Wikistorm, going from Wikipedia article to another until she realized that she had wasted a whole day filling her mind with random crap, instead of doing what she was actually supposed to do, like reading a chapter for class.

She tried to rack her brain for anything to give him, but her brain remained stubbornly blank. With each second that ticked by, the silence became more tense for everyone. The only one that didn't seem uncomfortable was Professor Maxwell. He seemed to almost delight in the situation he created.

Finally, he spoke again, "I see from the look on your face that the answer is no. Do keep in mind that I do not tolerate slackers in my class. Do try to be better prepared next time."

As he talked, she slumped in her seat, wishing that everyone would just stop looking at her. After a moment or two, she got her wish. The students slowly turned away from her and focused on the professor, making sure that they wouldn't be the next to be caught off guard.

A few hours later, Karyna was in the library. She was determined to focus on studying and not get distracted. She had to catch up before she got into real trouble with Professor Maxwell. She heard horror stories about that man.

Settling in one of the seats with the textbook open in front of her and a dog-eared notebook next to it, she chewed on the capped end of a pen, willing herself to focus on the lesson.

A loud thump startled her. Looking around, she saw a leather-bound book on the table next to her. Raising her dark eyes, she blinked at the sight of the man before her. The guy looked young. Baby-faced even. Dark eyes and dark hair. What really stuck out was how he dressed. He looked a bit old fashioned and proper. Not like most of the guys around here. They tended to live in sloppy t-shirts and baggy jeans. This guy looked like he was going to church service.

As she continued to stare at him with a confused expression, he gave her a sheepish smile. "Sorry about that. The book got away from me. One would think that it didn't want to be read."

Grabbing the book, she looked at the cover. "Local Urban Legends of Boston. Are you taking one of Professor Maxwell's classes?"

He rubbed the back of his neck with his hand while he chuckled, "Nah. I just love reading about the stuff. Not sure if I believe any of it, but they tend to be good tales."

She handed the book to him, "Most of them tend to have some grain of truth to them."

Then realizing that she hadn't introduced herself, she said, "By the way, I'm Karyna."

He took the book. "Donald Ninian. Book Wrangler. I take it from what you've said that you're a student of this professor?"

Karyna nodded. "Yeah. Professor Maxwell is the head of the Folklore department. He's tough, but he knows his stuff."

His brows raised up. "Folklore? Didn't know anyone would want to study that."

She gave a small smile. "I want to be a writer. This seemed to be the best thing for that. Study stories of the past and try to twist them into something new. Probably sounds silly to you."

He shook his head. "Nope. Makes perfect sense actually. The past is full of forgotten gems. Stories waiting to be explored and expand upon. That stuff keeps the past alive in a sense."

Karyna relaxed a little at his words. "That's exactly right. There are some stories that seem to be the same all over the world. Like some kind of collective memory. An example of this is that every culture seems to have a flood story."

He nodded in agreement. "Another one would be the Lady In White."

She paused and looked at him in confusion. "What do you mean?"

The man reached out to grab a nearby chair and sat in it while leaning closer to her. "You've never heard of the Lady In White?"

Scrunching her face while shrugging, she said, "The ghost chick that likes to hang out by a cemetery in Chicago?"

Donald laughed and shook his head. "That's one specific Lady. The strange thing about Resurrection Mary is that they're pretty sure who she was when she was alive. There seem to be thousands of these ghost ladies. From what I can tell, they seem to usually haunt a road. They also seem to almost always be referred to as Mary."

She snorted at that. "That's really not a shocker. It's a generic girl's name. Anyone could be Mary."

He grinned, "This is true. Still, even Boston has its own Lady In White. It's just her name isn't Mary but Marjorie. Close enough, I guess. She tends to haunt Beacon Hill."

Karyna leaned a little closer while asking, "What's her story?"

He pushed the leather book over to her. "You might need this book more than me. Take it."

Her fingers brushed the aged cover. "Are you sure?"

Donald grinned. "Yep. I can get it another time. Just let me know what you think. Deal?"

Taking the book, she shrugged. "Deal."

Chapter 3: The Mystery

Karyna felt pretty proud a few days later. She had completed reading the assignments and even took notes. Of course, since she was prepared, Professor Maxwell didn't call on her. Typical. Still, it was better than being caught unprepared.

After class, she packed her battered bag and walked up to the professor's desk, waiting her turn to talk to him about something. She had read the book that Donald had given her. What was odd was that it hadn't been a library book. When she went to check it out, Mrs. Montgomery had given her an annoyed look and told her that she didn't need the library's permission to read it. Karyna didn't know what to make of that. Why did Donald act like he was checking out the book? The next question was how was she going to find him once she finished the thing? It wasn't like they exchanged phone numbers. Then there was the story he wanted her to read. She had a lot of questions, and Professor Maxwell seemed to be the best person to answer those.

When it was finally her turn, she saw the look of surprise on his face. This had actually been the first time Karyna had stayed after class for anything. She was more of a bolter. If she had a question about the assignments, she would usually email him, so she didn't take his shocked expression personally.

She cleared her throat before saying, "I have a strange situation. Something tells me that you're the only one that can help me with this."

He raised a brow. "Rather melodramatic. Don't you think, Miss Thorpe?"

Bracing herself, she continued, "What do you know about Marjorie Dyer?"

She watched as his eyes widened while he stilled. If she didn't know any better, she would say that he was afraid. It didn't make sense. Why would something like this scare him?

Her thoughts were interrupted when he asked, "How do you know that name?"

Reaching into her bag, she dug around for a moment before she pulled out the leather bound book and held it out to him. He looked at it, but didn't take it, just stared at it as if it was a snake about ready to strike out; so she was left feeling awkward while she had the book between them.

As he kept staring at the book, she said, "How I got the book is also strange. Want to hear it, or am I going to keep holding this book feeling like an idiot?"

There was finally some understanding in his bright blue eyes. Looking around, he seemed to be checking to see if there was anyone else watching. Karyna had made sure to be the last one to get in line, so they were alone in the classroom. When he realized this, he seemed to relax for a moment or two.

Standing up, he grabbed his briefcase and motioned her with his hand. "Come. This would be better if we talked in my office."

Looking down at the book that was still in her hand, she shoved it back in her bag and shrugged, not really happy with going into his office. In her mind, it meant that this was bigger than she realized. That could not be good.

A few minutes later, they were in his office. It wasn't the usual explosion of papers and books like most of the professors she knew. It wasn't tidy either. The best words that she could use to describe it was that the office looked lived in. One could tell that he spent a lot of time here.

When he sat down behind his desk, he motioned for her to give him the book. She grabbed it out of her bag again before sitting down and handing it to him. Silently, she watched him as he flipped through the pages. The man had a damn good poker face. She couldn't pick up on anything. It was like his face was made of stone.

Finally, setting the book down, he folded his hands and asked, "How did you get this book?"

With a shrug, she said, "Some guy named Donald Ninian bumped into me in the library and gave it to me. It was weird because he made it seem as though he was going to check it out. It surprised me when I found out that it wasn't a library book."

His eyes widened, "That's impossible. Donald Ninian has been dead for over ninety years."

She tilted her head to the side while saying, "Well, this Donald Ninian wasn't dead. Just looked a little overdressed for an afternoon study session. Pretty sure dead guys don't wander around flinging books at people for a conversation starter."

Professor Maxwell snorted. "You'd be surprised."

He then tapped the cover with his index finger. "This book shouldn't exist anymore. I burnt it twenty years ago."

Karyna frowned. "It could be a different copy."

He opened the book and flipped to the second to last page. He then pointed to a doodle of a daisy with the initials M.M. next to it. She had seen that when she first read it but didn't think anything about it. Now, it seemed that there was way more going on.

He calmly said, "Mallory Maxwell was my older sister. Sadly, thirty years ago this book and Donald Ninian brought about her death. I am sure you can now understand my concern."

She looked down at the book and then back at him. "I would really like to know what I got dragged into."

Professor Maxwell nodded. "That is a valid request. The simple answer would be nothing good. I'm sure you would like more information than that."

She raised her brow and crossed her arms. "Naturally."

Running his fingers through his gray hair before answering, he said, "I assure you that this is not easy for me. I swore to myself that I would never talk about what happened to Mallory. Not just because I lost my sister."

Karyna waited quietly until he was ready to continue.

"I honestly don't know where to start," he said. "My sister was a bright sweet woman that liked to paint daisies and woodland scenes. The change seemed sudden. She became secretive, withdrawn. Her paintings took a darker turn. They seemed to be more nightmarish than the bright things she used to create. My parents thought she was going through a phase. I knew differently."

Standing up, he went to a nearby bookshelf. He moved a few things so there was a space that he could reach the back. He came back holding a battered book. It looked like one of those diaries with the flimsy locks that every woman seemed to get when they were young. Karyna used hers for her first attempt at a story. This one had a daisy print on the cover and was bent at the edges.

He gestured to the book with his other hand. "She loved daisies. Said how it was impossible to have a bad day with a daisy around."

Flipping through the worn pages, he then stopped, looking at the writing for a moment. His fingers brushed against the page, as if he could bring forth the past. It was rather heartbreaking to watch. She felt as though she was intruding on a private moment.

When she shifted, he looked up. "Forgive me. Something like this is never easy. Doesn't matter how much time has passed."

Sitting back down, he continued, "I was the typical younger brother. Snooping into things I shouldn't have. Like her diary. In the beginning, it was typical teenage stuff. She wrote about school, friends, worries about the future. Then things took a more sinister turn. She wrote about nightmares and the feeling of being followed. It all seemed to start when she met a gentleman at an art show. His name was also Donald Ninian. She even drew what she saw in her diary."

With those words, he flipped the diary, so she could see the page. In a rough pencil sketch was what looked like a woman in a long flowing dress walking down a lane. That in itself was bad. It was the woman's eyes that sent chills down Karyna's spine. There was so much rage and pain looking back from the page. It made the sketch horrific to look at.

She looked back at him. "What does this have to do with Marjorie Dyer?"

Maxwell tapped his index finger to the drawing. "That is Marjorie Dyer. I'm certain. My sister never really paid attention to stories or history. This was also before the Internet. Legends didn't travel as quickly or as far back then. Until Ninian, she never had known about The Cursed Woman of Beacon Hill."

Karyna frowned. "She wasn't called that in the book."

He leaned back and sighed. "No, but that's what those who do know about her call her. Nothing good comes from her. The book gives you the bare bones of the story. It tells of a woman that loved unwisely and committed suicide because of it. What it does not tell you is that anyone that comes into contact with her either dies or leads a cursed life. There are no happy endings with this tale."

Thinking back on what she had read, she had to admit that he was right. There really hadn't been much detail in the book about what happened. It mostly hinted that she had a forbidden love affair and that she was found dead at the grave of Samuel Sewall at Granary Burying Ground. It didn't explain why she was at a cemetery at night. It didn't even tell how Marjorie died. Just that she was found dead by a caretaker. Even the grave didn't seem to give any clues. Sewall had been a judge during the Salem witch trials, the only one to apologize, and admit that it had been wrong. That was it. There was nothing really connecting Marjorie to the repentant judge. Most legends and ghost stories did at least go into detail about why the love was forbidden. Not this one. It read more like a generic blurb than a legend. It was why Karyna came to Maxwell, wanting to know how this story could not be more well known.

Karyna quietly asked, "How did your sister die?"

Maxwell looked down at the worn diary. "Inconclusive. That's the official word. Just a legal term for the fact they have no clue. There are theories though. Some fantastical and some even insulting."

Leaning forward, she asked, "And what do you think?"

He looked up in shock. "I don't have a theory because I know. I followed her that night and saw it all happen." Shaking his head, he went on, "I've said too much. You need to walk away from this and pretend that you never heard about Marjorie Dyer."

She answered while frowning, "I can't. Donald Ninian gave me that book. I'm supposed to meet up with him again to tell him my thoughts. I don't think he'll take no for an answer."

The professor nodded. "Forgive me. You're absolutely correct. I don't know why, but you seemed to already be chosen for the next chapter of this tragedy. I had hoped that it had ended with my sister. Foolish. I know."

With those words, he gave her the diary. "I don't know how much help it will be. I studied it for most of my life, and I still can't figure it out. Maybe you can understand and solve the puzzle."

Karyna looked down at the book in her hand. "That's it? I have to do this alone?"

His brows furrowed as his mouth twisted into a frown. "Good heavens, no. I am not abandoning you to face the same fate as my sister alone. I just thought the diary would serve you better. Forgive me. I seem to be fumbling this horribly."

Her shoulders sagged as she sighed. "I get it. Pretty much just sashayed up to you and pulled the proverbial rug from under you. Anyone would be out of sorts."

Raising a brow, he said, "I believe you were more meandering than sashaying."

She narrowed her eyes as she studied him, trying to figure out if he was joking or not. When she saw a slight twitch of his lips, she decided that he had been trying to joke. It was hard to tell with him because he had always seemed serious in class. Felt weird that he was trying to joke now. She guessed that he was trying to make her feel better. Karyna decided that it would be kinder to not let him know that he failed miserably.

She looked back up at him. "First things first. We need to find what we can about Marjorie Dyer. Figure out what happened to her. That should help us unravel this mystery."

Karyna then paused before asking him, "How much time do I have?"

He shrugged. "A month. Maybe two. Give or take. I think as long as Ninian doesn't come back to ask you questions, we have time. Unfortunately, this is not an exact science. I can only go with the information that's available. As you can tell, there is not much."

With a worried expression, she looked down at the tattered diary. "Guess we better get started then."

Chapter 4: Unraveled Threads

The most frustrating thing about trying to find the source of an urban legend is that so many people claim to know how it all started. Even though they had a name, there was still a lot of crap to sift through. If Karyna didn't know better, she would think that Marjorie didn't want her story to be known.

The diary helped somewhat. Mallory was as the professor described her. Sweet and upbeat. Always trying to see the good in everyone. The run in with Ninian was a lot like Karyna's. Random and charming. She even noticed that Mallory mentioned how he seemed to have an old fashioned vibe to him. As though he was from a different time. There was even a sketch of him. When Karyna looked at it, the sense of dread settled in the pit of her stomach. She couldn't tell what role Ninian played, but she figured that he was an important part of this mystery.

She noticed that it hadn't taken Ninian that long to get back to Mallory. Just three days, from what was written in the diary.

That made Karyna and Maxwell nervous. They couldn't tell if it was a good thing or a bad thing that this guy hadn't started on the next part of this. It made her wonder if there was something different about this situation. She tried to ask Maxwell about it, but he would shut down when she tried to bring up Mallory. She could sympathize that it was a painful subject, but she needed all the information she could get before she ended up like his sister, Until she felt she could push more, Karyna stuck to the diary, hoping that it would give some clue as to why this was happening. So far, she didn't even have a theory. That was worrisome because she could usually think of some kind of theory. This time? Nothing. It was almost like there was a block in her mind.

From what she could tell from the diary, once Ninian came back, Mallory started to slide into a kind of madness. She would write that she felt like she was being watched, even when she was alone. Then there were the nightmares. From what Karyna could tell, they seemed to play on Mallory's fears of not being good enough and being left behind. Common fears, but the nightmares seemed to make them ten times worse. She didn't know how anyone could handle being plagued with such intense horrific dreams night after night. From the diary, she could tell that Mallory couldn't. The handwriting would become more erratic until it was illegible. At the end, it was just one phrase written over and over. Some of the words looked like the pen had been digging into the page while being written. It made it more real to Karyna. Not that it didn't feel that way before, just that she was now holding proof of what she could experience if they couldn't solve this mystery.

Something told her that once Ninian came back, it might be too late for her. Of course, trying to figure out what really happened to Marjorie Dyer was turning out to be just as complicated as Maxwell said it would. She had hoped that they would be able to find something. Even a footnote would have made her feel better. No. Instead, it seemed that Marjorie didn't make an impact until after her death. They were even having problems locating her grave. If she hadn't read the diary, Karyna would have doubted that Marjorie had existed.

Leaning forward, she sighed and rested her head on the library table. Closing her eyes, she tried to think on what the next move would be. From the few clues they had been able to find, Dyer had been well off. So, their next step might be to go to all the cemeteries near Beacon Hill and look at each grave to see if they could find hers. It was the best plan they had. From there, they might be able to piece the puzzle together. Hopes weren't high, though.

She didn't realize that she had fallen asleep until she became aware that she was walking down a cobblestone street. She recognized it as a street near Old Granary. Looking around, she saw that the streetlights were lit with candles. It gave the area an eerie quality. Not that it needed any help. The place was creepy at night with the silence pressing around her. The silence actually made her head hurt, as though her ears were trying to pop but couldn't.

Suddenly, she heard a rustling sound. Turning her head, she saw the figure in Mallory's sketch walking towards her. Marjorie Dyer was pure white from her clothes to her skin. Her eyes and hair seemed to be made from darkness. She was a walking nightmare, and she was slowly coming towards Karyna. Karyna froze where she stood, unable to move, her breath coming out in ice puffs.

The woman looked at her, not saying a word. With eyes filled with rage, the dead woman reached out and grabbed hold of her throat. She could feel ice cold bony fingers pressing into her skin. The touch was so cold that it felt like it burned, causing Karyna to scream.

Snapping her eyes open, she looked around. Seeing that no one was paying attention, she sighed with relief. It was just a dream. She was safe in the library. Well, as safe as she could be in this situation. Her breath slowed as she focused on the fact that it was a dream. Not sure what it meant. In Mallory's diary, the dreams didn't start until after Ninian came back. She worried that this might mean something had changed since Mallory's death, but Karyna was not sure what it could be. Maxwell was still closed off when it came to his sister's death. It was frustrating, but she got it. She just had to hope that he would breakdown and start sharing. There could be something important that she needed to know. Her life depended on figuring this out, and the sooner the better.

As she started gathering her books, she heard a sound. Turning her head, she saw him. Her stomach dropped. Donald Ninian looked exactly the same as last time. He even had the same smile. Actually, no. The smile was sharper, like that of a predator that was closing in on its prey. Karyna had a feeling that she was the prey.

He leaned toward her with that sharp smile still on his face. "Well, well. I wasn't expecting this. Congratulations. You actually managed to surprise me. That hasn't happened in a long time. Can't wait to see what this means. Most exciting."

She leaned back in an attempt to keep as much space as possible between them. "Not for me, it's not. What's in this for you?"

He tilted his head a little to the side before answering. "That's for me to know and you to maybe figure out. I have to admit, I wasn't expecting you to get this far. Maybe I have finally picked a smart one. Try not to disappoint."

Her eyes widened at his words. The blatant insult made her bristle, but she kept still. She had no idea what the rules were. Even so, she felt that lashing out at him would not end well for her. Instead, her fingers dug into the wood of the desk, trying to keep herself from doing something stupid.

Finally, she whispered, "What are you?"

The sharp smile was back. "Clever girl. I'll leave that for you to puzzle out. Until then, I'll see you in your dreams."

One moment he was there grinning at her with that sharp edge smile. The next he was gone, as if he had never been there. Sitting there stunned for a moment, she tried to calm her breathing. Soon her mind started working. She needed to find Maxwell and talk to him about what happened. Karyna felt that she was just given a big piece of the puzzle. She simply had to figure out what it was first. Hopefully, the professor would be able to help her with that.

Grabbing her notes and books, she left to find the professor. Time was running out, and it seemed that the game was different than before. Something told her that it wasn't in her favor.

Chapter 5: And the Clock Ticks On

Stumbling while trying to walk to her next class, she caught herself before she fell down. Her books shifted, but fortunately, she didn't drop anything. It was another example of needing to get some sleep. She gave it another day or two before she tried again. If she was lucky, she could get a whole two hours before waking up screaming.

It had been a few weeks since she had that strange talk with Ninian, and she was exhausted. The nightmares were horrific. It wasn't that they were bloody. In a way, they were tame. What was so terrifying about the dreams was that there was a strong sense of Karyna losing herself. In her mind, there was nothing worse. Because of the dreams, she had been trying to avoid sleeping as much as she could. It wasn't the best plan, but it was all she had.

Straightening up while deciding if class was worth the effort, she stopped as she saw Professor Maxwell coming toward her.

They had talked once right after her encounter with Ninian. After a few frustrating hours, they decided the only thing that had changed was the fact she had read Mallory's diary. Because of that, she knew what was going to happen. Just because she knew, didn't make it easier to deal with. The dark circles under her eyes were a testament to that. After, they had avoided each other. She understood why he was avoiding her. He didn't want to see her end up like his sister. She was avoiding him because she didn't see this ending well at all, and keeping him at a distance seemed kinder since he didn't get a choice when it came to his sister.

He stopped in front of her and simply said, "I found her."

Her eyes widened as she stared at him. Trying to process what he just said, her mouth hung open before snapping shut. Feeling herself shake, she tried not to cry. Hope. There was finally some hope.

He gave her a small smile. "I assume you don't mind ditching class."

Karyna shook her head. "No. Can we go now?"

He offered his arm. "I thought you'd never ask."

She wasn't sure how long it had been as they silently rode in the back of a cab, but she was surprised by where they ended up. Looking at the brick building with a frown, she turned to Maxwell with a questioning look, trying to figure out what they should do next, hoping he would take the lead.

He looked at her with a shrug. "Seems the Dyers were rather well off. When she died, they were able to place her body in the crypt. I'm sure there were some pockets lined to achieve that. From what I could find, the family was worried about the curious seekers. Understandable. She became a legend from the moment she died."

Karyna stared at him in stunned silence for a moment before responding. "That makes sense. It would also be why no one found her grave until now. How did you actually find her?"

He grinned. "I know someone on the Old North Church committee. They had been talking about the crypts underneath. Marjorie came up. Seems she is an unspoken celebrity to them, and they like their little secrets."

She frowned. "Did you have to promise anything to get them to tell you?"

He grinned even more, "You'd be amazed what doors flattery can open up for you. Come. Let's see what we can find out."

She looked back to the unadorned gray stone church. "What do you hope to find?"

He said, "Answers. If anything, we might her spirit here as well. She can't be wandering the streets of Beacon Hill all the time."

She raised a brow. "You know that for sure?"

He paused before answering. "More of a theory. Believe it or not, I actually don't know much about the habits of spirits. Still, this is something. Let's see where it will lead us."

She nodded and then took his offered arm. She would need to sleep soon, and she wasn't looking forward to it. Karyna glanced towards him before focusing on her steps. Dread started to build up in the pit of her stomach, making her wonder if she would ever be able to enjoy life without fear. She decided it would be best to dwell on that at another time. At the moment, they had more pressing questions to answer.

It was surprisingly easy to get into the old crypt area. Most people didn't seem to pay attention to them. Guess they had a little bit of good luck on their side. Hopefully, it wouldn't tilt the other way anytime soon.

It was tidy but still gloomy. Even without dust, crypts couldn't be cheerful. Marjorie's body was in the back, almost as if it was hiding. It was rather plain, just a plaque with her name with the date of her birth and the date of her death. Nothing that really stuck out until the inscription.

Leaning closer, Karyna read, "May she always bear the burden of her actions, and the consequences be her curse."

She then looked up toward Maxwell. "It doesn't sound like she was mourned. What could she have done to have this as her epitaph?"

He was staring at the words carved in stone as he said, "People were less forgiving back then when it came to scandal. Her unforgivable sin was that she created a sensation with how she died. Not some wasting disease. She was not a modest young miss that discreetly passes on at home. No. She was bold and died suddenly at Sewall's grave. Well, bold for the early nineteenth century. I'm sure people today would think it more quaint than dramatic. "

She looked back at the tomb. "It was a tragedy, but I can't believe that they would think this was unforgivable."

He said, "Doesn't matter. She did, and so she is here instead of with her family. Look around. She is the only Dyer here. They cut her from the family in death. With how hard it's been to find anything solid to prove that she existed, they probably tried to erase anything they could about her being real."

Karyna still stared at the tomb "There has to be more to it than that. I can't believe her family could be so heartless about losing a family member."

Still, suicide was frowned upon even today. Back then, it was a major scandal. It would make sense that her family would try to shove her into the shadows. It would also explain the cruel epitaph. Didn't make it right.

As she was thinking this, she brushed her fingers along the cold words. There was a strange sensation that made her feel dizzy. Closing her eyes for a moment, she opened them and was horrified by what she saw. It seemed that she was now in the crypt, lying down on the cold stone, surrounded by darkness. Before she could scream, she felt something shift next to her, causing her to still and hold her breath, hoping that whatever this was would stop soon. She did not get that wish. Suddenly, she was face-to-face with a decaying face looming over her. It took a second or two for her to realize that it was Marjorie. The dead woman's face looked like something from a Stephen King novel. The way her skin was hanging off made her look like she was giving a ghoulish grin as she lowered her face until it was right next to Karyna's. She could smell the stench of rotting meat. Marjorie made a hissing sound, and Karyna started to scream and flail, trying to break out of the stone grave.

Feeling someone shaking her, she opened her eyes and saw Maxwell looking at her with concern. With jerky motions, she looked around, trying to control her body shaking. She was still beside her professor, not trapped in a stone prison with a rotting corpse. In that moment, she broke down and started crying. It was too much. They didn't have any clue how to stop this. What was worse, they didn't know what this was.

In the next moment, she felt arms wrap around her, giving her comfort. In a soft voice, he said, "We'll figure this out. You're not alone."

It was something at least. She just clung to Maxwell, until she cried herself out. Even after that, she held on, terrified that if she let go, the thing in the tomb would try and pull her back and trap her there.

As she kept her arms wrapped around him, she wondered if they would figure things out like he said. Keeping silent, she just nodded her head. It was better to let one of them have hope. She would let him have it. While she made that promise, the ticking of his Rolex watch reminded her that time was running out.

Chapter 6: Ghost of Our Minds

A few days after visiting Old North, Karyna unraveled more. She had been trying to keep a journal like Mallory. The problem was that she was worried about what would happen to the journal after she met her end. The most logical thought was that it would go to Maxwell. He might be able to help the next girl, if there was one.

That thought stilled her pen. She hoped there wouldn't be another girl after this. Brushing some of her dark hair from her face, she flipped through Mallory's diary again, trying to see if there was any clue as to how she could stop this. She might not be able to save herself, but maybe she could break the chain so that it wouldn't continue.

Finally, she found a passage that she was looking for in the diary. Karyna didn't know if the idea would work, but it was worth a shot. She just needed to keep it together long enough.

Just then, she felt the air in the room change. Looking up, she saw Marjorie staring at her. Usually, when she saw the dead woman, she felt red hot rage directed at her. It scared her. It made her wonder if Marjorie was a victim. She didn't seem to act like she wanted anyone's help. It brought up the question of what Ninian's role was in all of this. Not a nice one was the only answer her exhausted mind could think up.

This time, Marjorie smiled as if she found out something wonderful. Still, she was silent. Karyna had tried to talk to her in the beginning when she started dreaming about her. That seemed to agitate the dead woman further, so she learned to be silent and wait to see what would happen. After a minute, the spirit faded as if she had never been there. There were times she wondered if maybe she was imagining all of this and Maxwell was humoring her. She wouldn't blame him. Except for the crypt at Old North, this was the first time she had seen Marjorie somewhere else besides in her nightmares. This felt different. Marjorie was smiling instead of glaring in rage.

Glancing back at the discarded diary, Karyna then rested her head on her knees. Closing her eyes, she tried to fight back the tears. They wouldn't help. She needed to do something. Lifting her head back up, she looked at the diary again, and thought on what she read before the spirit appeared. It took just a moment but her decision made, she knew that she had one more thing to do before she acted on it.

Getting up, she reached for the phone and dialed Maxwell's number, "I'm sorry. I know how this is going to end, and it's not going to be pretty. I don't blame you, so don't blame yourself. This wasn't your fault. Thank you, and I hope you find happiness. Goodbye."

She quickly ended the call, not knowing if she had actually gotten a hold of him or had been talking to his voicemail. It didn't matter. One way or another, Maxwell would know. Glancing at the clock next to her bed, she knew that she didn't have much time. He would try to stop her. She couldn't allow him to do that. With that thought, she dropped her phone on the floor, not caring that it shattered. All that mattered was her mission. Walking out of her dorm room, she left the door open. If things went the way she expected, she wouldn't be coming back.

She didn't know how much time passed as she walked to the cemetery, but she found herself standing in front of Sewall's grave. The place where all this really started with Marjorie's death. Part of her was surprised that she was able to get in after dark, but after all that had happened, that was the least shocking thing.

Looking around, she wasn't sure what she was waiting for until she heard it. The rustling of soft material and light steps on cobblestone. Turning around slowly, she came face to face with Marjorie. The woman was smiling. It wasn't a warm smile and yet strangely gleeful. It made Karyna want to run.

Marjorie's voice was like a harsh winter wind. "Do you agree?"

Karyna took a breath before answering. "Will I be the last, if I do this?"

The spirit tilted her head as if in thought before answering, "As long as you do your part, no others will be sought out. Do you agree now?"

With a nod of her head, Karyna said, "I agree."

As the words left her lips, she felt Marjorie's cold fingers wrap around her throat. The sensation was so painful, it caused her to scream as tears fell down her cheeks. Soon, everything went dark.

Chapter 7: Devil In the Details

Maxwell had been foolish and rushed over to Karyna's dorm apartment when she hung up. He barely remembered the key she gave him on his last visit to go over their research. It seemed like she gave it to him as an afterthought, but now the feeling of dread settled heavily on his shoulders. The fear that he let her down like he let Mallory down swirled around in his mind.

When he got there and used the key, he saw Mallory's diary on the floor. Next to it was another journal. Quickly, he realized that it was Karyna's. Flipping through the pages, his eyes widened at what he read. Grabbing Mallory's diary off the floor, he flipped through those pages before he found what he was looking for. He stood staring at the words on the page before dropping it and running out of the room, fearful that he was too late.

He made it to Sewall's grave out of breath. Looking around, he didn't see anyone. He hoped that he made it in time to stop

Karyna, but a part in the back of his mind whispered that he failed again.

A chuckle from the shadows had him turn around and ask, "Where is she? Where's Karyna?"

The man that went by the name of Donald Ninian walked out of the darkness with a smile on his lips. "Too late again. Must be disheartening. First you failed your sister, and now innocent Karyna. I have to say that she surprised me. Your sister figured it out but didn't agree. Karyna did. The deal is done. There is nothing left for you to do. No damsels to save. No riddles to unravel. Go home and drown in your failure. It's what you do best, Boy!"

Maxwell shook his head, "I might not have been able to save Mallory, but Karyna is not lost. Not yet. I won't give up."

Ninian moved closer. His dark eyes flashed black for a second. It was so quick that one might have thought it was a shadow crossing his face. The smile sharpened as he looked at the other man, like he had heard a good joke.

He then said to Maxwell, "Stubborn until the end. I like that. See you around, Boy. I'm sure this won't be the last time we meet."

With that, Ninian faded into the shadows. Maxwell looked at the spot with some confusion, not knowing what he should do next.

Turning around, he saw Marjorie Dyer smiling at him. She looked different, more alive, no longer like a ghost that she should be.

She twirled a little before she said, "I never thought this would happen. I am happy that she agreed. The others were so simple. Never understood a thing."

He frowned. "One of those simple ones was my sister, Madam. What have you done?"

She faced him and shrugged a shoulder. "Found my freedom. The deal was made. She agreed. I'm sure she'll adjust. After all, I did."

With that, she walked away from him, almost skipping. He couldn't move, the anger was so strong. It was then he heard a soft rustle of material. Slowly turning around, he saw her. Karyna was an ashy color that wasn't helped by the long white dress she wore. As he stared at her, he felt his cheeks wet from the tears falling. He watched her in silence because he didn't know what to say.

She moved towards him. "Do I know you? You seem familiar."

In a rough voice he answered, "Maxwell. I'm Maxwell. Do you remember what happened, Karyna?"

She looked at him with confusion. "Karyna? I thought my name was Mary. It seemed that anyone like me is named Mary."

He asked, "Like you?"

She tilted her head. "I'm the Lady In White. I'm sure you've heard of the legends."

She didn't even wait for his response. Turning a little, she walked toward the cemetery's gates and faded into the darkness. Maxwell just stared as she disappeared, the sound of Ninian's laughter ringing in his ears.

Chapter 8: Wanderings

Sometimes I remember talking to Maxwell by Sewall's grave. I don't know why he called me that strange name. Mary seemed more logical. Still, he saw me. That was something. I was unsure as to what that could mean. I couldn't go back to ask him. I couldn't leave the little stretch in Beacon Hill. Hopefully, one day I will see him again. He seemed rather nice, though sad. I understood sadness. I just can't remember why.

There were times I would see another man. He had a sharp smile. It was unnerving. When he appears, I try to avoid him. He would just laugh and say how a deal was a deal. I would never ask him. It was wiser to stay far from him. I would figure out how to break this curse. I knew I could. Until then, I would wander the streets and hope that I can free myself. Until then, I was just another Lady In White reminding the living that tragedy walks among them.

Karolyne Cronin

A hyperactive woman with a dark imagination. Karolyne Cronin spins nightmares into entertainment for the world.

Find her online at www.KarolyneCronin.com or on Facebook at Karolyne Cronin-Author.

Mystick Tea

By Mimi Schweid

THE HANGED MAN.

"I really hate faeries," Veronica says with a scowl as she walks inside her apartment, hanging her keys up on the hook near the door. She leans against the wall as she slips off her boots and looks up at her girlfriend Krysten, waiting for her comment. Krysten was taller than she was and even more so in the high heels she wore. It was just one of the many things she loved about her girlfriend. Even when she was feeling moody because they were just in the elevator with her least favorite neighbors.

"You know that's a really offensive term." Krysten slips off her heels with the dancer's grace Veronica both loved and envied. Krysten was even graceful after the handful of Mimosa's they just had at brunch. "I thought you didn't use slurs like that Vee."

"No Krysten, we've been over this," Veronica's tone is harsher than she intends, and she plans on apologizing for it later tonight, "when I'm talking about faeries, I don't mean it that way." Veronica pushes off the wall and heads towards the kitchen. "And it's more than just general hatred. It's a passionate dislike."

Throughout the apartment that the couple shared were various crystals for things such as protection, clear communication, wealth, and stones to help with anxiety. Veronica wasn't only a proud lesbian but an equally as proud witch. This was not a secret between Veronica and Krysten, but she kept certain things to herself, feeling that it would be a burden for her loving girlfriend. Her girlfriend that danced for various Broadway shows all while she danced her way into Veronica's heart.

Krysten follows Veronica, grabs a spoon out of one of the drawers before she makes a beeline for the fridge, pulling out a jar of Nutella, and sits at the kitchen table. She gives Veronica a serious look before speaking once again, "You always skirt around as to why you hate faeries. I've been putting two and two together, and if I'm right, and I'm honestly hoping I'm not, please don't be mad."

Veronica does her best to act as if she didn't notice the look Krysten had given her and instead, sets up her tea pot, filling it with water and turns it on at the stove. Chamomile tea would ease her nerves for where this conversation was headed. More booze wouldn't help the situation, even if it was tempting. "Go on."

"Faeries hurt you as a child somehow, or someone else close to you. Possibly your little sister, the one in the photos you keep in the purple photo album in the back of the closet. I've only seen three pictures of her though, so that's why I think it's her more than you. One from Halloween of you two dressed up as Valkyries, one of you two at summer camp, and one from a birthday party." Krysten takes a quick pause to open the jar of Nutella and eats more before continuing, "I think faeries took your sister from you. And that the ones that live above us are why you've been adding crystals into my bags and putting spells on all my clothes while I'm in the shower or at rehearsal."

"Out of all the women in New York, how did I end up with the beautiful dancer that is freakishly astute?" Veronica asks in that way that was both a question and a fact. The tea pot starts to hiss, and she plucks out two mugs from her cabinet that she had claimed as the Tea Cabinet. "I wish you weren't right either, but I can't lie to you about that. It's not fair when I know you are saying it out of the kindness of your heart."

Veronica pours them both a mug full of Chamomile tea before she places them lightly on the table. As she sits down, she reaches across the table to hold Krysten's free hand that isn't holding the Nutella. Veronica squeezes it, for support and because she knows her hands will shake otherwise. Or that she'd make things short circuit in the kitchen again or somehow animate all the appliances like she used to do in college when she was feeling nervous. With her free hand, she takes a sip of her tea, puts it back down, and lets out a breath. This wasn't going to be easy to say, but things like this never were. Opening that part of your soul that you try to hide because of the shame, the rage, and the pain that makes you want revenge. Anger wasn't an emotion she cared to show. She knew it wasn't healthy to hide it either, but she was worried as to how her power would show her feelings. Taking another sip of tea, she allows herself one more second to collect her thoughts before she speaks.

"Her name was Miriam. She was ten years old, and I was eighteen when it happened. We were at our family's lake house for the summer. She was swimming, and I was sitting at the dock keeping an eye out for her while our parents were out at the store. I can still remember the sound of her laughter before the Nixies came. Three of them circled her in the water, holding their hands and chanting. She didn't scream, she sang with them, and when I realized what was happening, that these things just appeared out of nowhere and wanted my sister, I tried to move, and I couldn't. They had an allure about them, like vampires but different. I knew this, every cell in my body knew this, and I couldn't do a thing. I couldn't move. And even now, no matter what I do or who helps me with the spell work, I can't find her."

Veronica lets go of Krysten's hand and places both of her hands on the table as she leans back in her chair, "My parents, as you know, kind souls that they are, disinherited me for it. Blaming me for not using my magick to save her, even though I tried to fight it, the pull they had on me, but it didn't work, and Miriam's been gone ever since." Veronica snatches her mug up again and drinks deeply, not caring that it burns her throat the entire time.

"I feel like we're going to need something stronger than tea to make this conversation less painful." Krysten says, putting the Nutella down. She wishes she could make it all better, wishes that she could do some kind of magick to ease the pain, but she knows, (she's read dozens of the books that Veronica has scattered throughout the apartment), that magick can't help this kind of pain, that the loss is something both useful for magick but still emotionally crippling. Krysten knows that all she can truly do is this, be present for Veronica. To help her in any way that she can, by loving her, by supporting her, and by avoiding the neighbors upstairs.

"I love you, and I'm here for you. I appreciate all of what you are doing to keep me safe. All the little gifts and spells." Krysten gets up from her seat and gestures for Veronica to do the same. She waits for her to move before she pulls her into a tight hug, "I love you, and I will do all that I can to help you with the cards you've been dealt."

Veronica makes a noise, some cross between holding back a sob and a laugh. Honestly, just a hysterical noise that isn't that uncommon from her after heart-to-heart moments like these. She hugs Krysten tightly as she mutters, "I love you too. I'm grateful to have you in my life, and I promise I won't go off on some revenge kick."

"Damn, Vee." Krysten pulls away slightly to look down at Veronica. "Why'd you have to go and say that? I know you are big overall on the concept of the 'do no harm to others' thing, but this is something else. This is something I can help you with."

"You are helping. Because if you said 'let's go get revenge,' we will both end up dead. I want revenge for Miriam, and I'll get it someday. It's not something I can let go, but it's also not worth the consequences. An outright attack against the Nixies would cause more than just a few Faeries to move into the apartment building."

Veronica leaves her hands wrapped around Krysten's waist as she speaks, looking up at Krysten with love and pain, but more love than anything. "I know they keep an eye on me, on us, to see what I do, and if I were to lash out, you would be hurt. And I can't risk that. I know it's not just my decision to make, but this conversation, this is something I've needed to say for years. I'm sorry I've been hiding it from you for so long, and I'm even more sorry that just seeing some of them in the elevator brought it all out of me. I never planned on telling you this way."

"Sometimes the right time is over tea and Nutella," Krysten says with a sly smirk, "All that matters right now is that we love each other. We can make it through this painful reveal. You've helped me with my cousin. I can and will help you through this."

"Moments like these, when you can say the sweetest things, even while filled with Mimosa and Nutella, are just one of the many that continue to make me fall in love with you every day." Veronica smiles, a soft, sad smile but a smile, nevertheless. She stands on her toes and kisses Krysten tenderly.

Veronica didn't believe in love at first sight. She didn't care for love potions, but did enjoy self-care rituals. The thing Veronica did believe in, magick or otherwise, since the moment she met Krysten, was that Krysten was special. That no matter what happened between the two of them, they would be important to one another. Romantic or otherwise, Krysten would always be a part of her life and vice versa.

Like every kiss they shared, Veronica was left breathless and grateful for whatever powers above helped align them together. They balanced one another out and helped keep each other calm. Veronica felt it in her bones, magick or no magick, that no matter how much she mourned Miriam, the thing she needed to do was just this. Surround herself with the love of her life. That love like this would keep her safe from all the horrors that haunted her. Love and support like this would be the best revenge against the Nixie's that haunted her dreams. Love was its own special kind of mystick tea.

Weeks pass, and Veronica notices that someone is following her. It is a tall woman, fair skinned, blonde hair, and haunting green eyes. She is always dressed in all black and seemed amused whenever Veronica flips her off. The woman's ears are pointed, like an elf's, and she towers over every crowd she walks through.

Krysten had texted her earlier this morning to ask her to meet her at their first date spot when she is on break from class. It is a tiny cafe down in the Village, a few blocks from the dance studio she was teaching at when they had first met. Krysten had continued to teach the at the studio on the side for some extra money.

Not spotting Krysten yet, she grabs a seat facing the door so she can see when she arrives, and if the woman makes an appearance. No more than five minutes pass before the woman sits down in the empty seat across from Veronica.

"Hello Veronica, I thought now would be a better time than any to let you know that I can help you find your sister." Her long legs take up space under the tiny circular table. Her boot-clad feet tap Veronica's chair as she stretches out. Her hair is braided in a crown on top of her head with Raven feathers, and despite the summer heat, the woman is dressed head-to-toe in leather. She wears a corset-style shirt, a leather jacket, and pants with knee-high boots. Veronica notices several knives and feels that the woman was making sure she would notice them. It looks like something Veronica expected to see at a night club, minus the knives, but the woman doesn't seem to care or look the slightest bit uncomfortable. The smile on her face, however, seems forced.

"Listen lady, you've been following me for the past week. Why should I listen to a thing you have to say?" Despite her anger, Veronica keeps her voice down. She doesn't want to cause a scene in one of her favorite places to meet clients with. Placing her hands onto her lap, she casts a privacy spell. It would keep their conversation in a soundproof dome so that only the two of them could hear what they discuss.

"Because I've been following you for weeks, and it's important." The woman taps at the bubble with her right foot, and a tiny spark goes up, "obviously, or else you wouldn't waste magick out in public like this."

"The shop knows what I'm capable of, and since you've been following me, so do you." Veronica leans forward now, placing her hands-on top of the table. "Give me your name, and I'll decide if I can trust you."

"You can call me Zarith." The woman says, placing a hand on top of Veronica's, "I work for the Queen of Order, and she has decided that if you make me a potion that I need, she will help you with your sister dilemma."

"What happened to Miriam isn't a dilemma, Zarith. She was taken from me." Veronica pulls her hand away and narrows her eyes at Zarith, "If you work for the Queen of Order, why does she want me to help you with a potion? I know who she is and what she is capable of. That means I know who and what you are." Veronica sits back in her seat, momentarily looking away from Zarith to make sure that Krysten isn't at the coffee shop just yet. "If I make you a potion, I don't believe I'll ever be free of either of you."

"If you make me the potion, I can promise you that the Nixies that took your sister will be punished. I need the spell to find them, but your rage and grief at the loss of Miriam has made my task rather difficult."

"What type of potion do you need?" Veronica asks as Zarith's smile starts to change. It doesn't look forced any more, it looks like she was desperate. Nervous almost. Neither of these things seem real to Veronica but this is a tempting offer. It seems too good to be true. If she did this, would she really get Miriam back? Or would she just be getting Zarith to have the revenge that she knew she would always want. Zarith's comment about being unable to find Miriam makes her feel trapped, but she pushes back the feeling. Letting her emotions get in the way of this bizarre situation won't get her any real answers.

Zarith reaches into her pants pocket and pulls out a tiny envelope. "The sooner you get me this made, the sooner I can do my Queen's bidding and help you." Zarith stands up and stretches, cracking her back. "Be a dear and have it done by midnight tonight." She pats Veronica gingerly on her head.

"How do either of you know I'll agree to do this?" Veronica asks, hitting Zarith's hand away from her head as the soundproof bubble expands to Zarith's height.

"Because, despite your loving conversation with Krysten, I know what you truly desire." Zarith takes an onyx stone bracelet out of her pocket and slips it onto Veronica's hand, the same one she used to slap her hand away. She smiles again, and this one seems real. "Hold onto the bracelet, and say my name three times. I'll handle the rest." Zarith pokes at the bubble again, this time with her hand before she walks away, leaving Raven feathers in her wake.

Veronica lets out a shaky breath as the sounds of the coffee shop come back to life around her. The sounds of people talking and laughing, the sound of the espresso machine and the cash register make her feel normal for a split second. This feels like some sort of cosmic set up, that the powers-that-be that were so kind to her to give her Krysten seem ready to make her life difficult suddenly. This is something she feels she can handle, or at least something she can try to do if it brings Miriam back.

Veronica leans down to pocket one of the Raven feathers left in Zarith's absence, knowing it will be useful at some point, before she leans back in her seat and starts to read the potions ingredients.

It is a spell for invisibility, a spell she practically mastered after her parents disinherited her. Veronica had to sneak back into her own home to get her belongings before her parents got rid of everything she had owned. It hadn't been easy, but she managed to do it at eighteen and won't have trouble making the potion now at almost thirty. She keeps a stock of invisibility potions, things for fire blasts and little smoke bombs in her bag anyway, but making it fresh for Zarith is probably her best bet. Veronica isn't sure how she is going to mention this to Krysten, but she knows she will have to speak with her about this before she starts anything else.

Another hour passes and Veronica hasn't heard from Krysten which makes her think that Zarith has somehow sent the text. Letting out a sigh, she leaves the café in a rush to head home. As she walks to her apartment, she feels that for once she isn't being watched.

As Veronica opens the door, to the sound of Krysten's post work playlist blasting greets her ears. It is easy Pop music, and it makes her smile as she slips off her shoes despite all the loud thoughts in her head for the conversation she needs to have. While Veronica is relieved that Krysten had reacted so well to her talking about Miriam, she isn't sure how to tell her she's been stalked by a potential Grim Reaper and now was sort of offered a job.

"Hey babe, how was your day?" Krysten asks as Veronica walks into the kitchen. "I'm sorry I never got to meet you at the shop. One of my students, Terri twisted his ankle and I've been with them at the hospital until his parents were able to reach us. They're okay now though, thankfully."

"I'm sorry about Terri," Veronica says as she takes out some Lavender tea and starts to brew a fresh pot. "I was approached by a client at the café anyway," Veronica says as she starts to look through her Spells cabinet to see if she has everything fresh for later, "So it all worked out okay in the end, I guess."

"What do they need from you, and did you get a deposit this time?" Krysten leans against the counter as Veronica starts to take out three white candles, a Moonstone, and a bottle of salt.

"Not exactly." Veronica shuts the cabinet, looking briefly at her ingredients before she looks at Krysten, "I'm not sure if you've read any of my books on the Kings and Queens of the Realms. Long story short, don't be mad, but I was approached by a Grim Reaper that's been following me for the past few weeks to make her a spell to get Miriam back from the Nixies."

"No, I haven't read any of your books on the other Realms. I can't wrap my head around half of what you have. Now let me get this straight, you haven't even mentioned to me that someone's been following you, and now you want to work with that same person? Doesn't this make you uncomfortable or uneasy?"

"I feel uncomfortable and uneasy because I haven't been sure how to tell you. I didn't want you to be worried about this, when until today, they, Zarith, haven't even done anything other than be horrible at not being noticed." Veronica says this slowly. "I need to make Zarith an Invisibility potion by Midnight, and I can get Miriam back. I know it's risky, and possibly a stupid move, but if Zarith gets the Nixies, I technically haven't had my revenge, so that's kind of better, right?"

"I love you, but I don't understand your rationale right now, Veronica." Krysten pushes herself off of the counter and pulls Veronica into a tight hug, "I love you, I trust you, I want you to be at peace with Miriam, but is this really the right idea?"

"Probably not, but I'm scared to say no to this offer." Veronica hugs Krysten back, allowing herself to enjoy this peaceful moment. "I don't think I can say no to this either." Veronica pulls away slowly and shows off the Onyx bracelet, "She gave me this to reach her tonight at midnight. The spell won't take that long to make either."

"Are you sure this isn't a trick to, oh, I don't know, get collected by a Grim Reaper?" Krysten half-shouts as she looks at the bracelet. It doesn't seem all that special to her, but then again, she isn't magickally inclined.

"They aren't like Fae or Demons; they have a strict code they follow. Especially because of who their boss is. The Queen of Order is a total bad-ass, but I wouldn't want to piss her off.

She's one of those all-powerful types no one can summon her or even speak to her unless you work for her. And even then, she won't always come when called." Veronica says this quickly, ignoring the fact Krysten was momentarily shouting. "I don't know if I can trust Zarith exactly, but this is a risk I will take. I just, I didn't want to do this without telling you. In case shit does hit the fan."

Krysten turns away from Veronica, pinches the bridge of her nose in a moment of silent contemplation before she turns to face Veronica again. "You've clearly made up your mind, and I can't exactly stop you. I don't think this is the right thing to do, but I don't know how to help either. I love you, and if you think this is the best option, I guess all I can say is that I hope, for both of our sakes, that it works out the way you want it to." She kisses Veronica on her forehead, "I trust you Vee. I know you'll be safe."

Hours pass, and the spell is complete. It is making the Moonstone into something that Zarith can channel to be invisible with the use of the white candles and Veronica's willpower. Out of all the spells she knows how to do, it is honestly one of the easiest. She adjusted it to work on her clothes when she was younger, and for whatever is about to happen tonight, she makes sure it works on Zarith's bracelet as well.

At eleven fifty, Veronica clears space in the living room to summon Zarith. Moonstone in one hand and bracelet still on, she focuses on the Queen of Order's woman of choice to get Veronica to do her bidding. As the clock strikes midnight,

Veronica begins her simple chant as she holds onto the bracelet. "Zarith, Zarith, Zarith."

Silence greets her for what seems like hours before she notices the change in the room. Raven feathers surround her in a hurricane of feathers, a perfect circle around her as she feels the room shake and change. She finds herself gasping for air as she no longer feels her carpeted floor but the unsteady feeling of being on the lake house dock. Balling her hands into tight fists, Veronica stops herself from chucking the Moonstone into the lake she has avoided for years.

"Zarith, this isn't funny." Veronica manages to say as the feathers stop swirling around her, and the woman finally shows herself. "Why am I here?"

"Because I needed you to get me to where it all happened." Zarith says with a shrug. Unlike in the café, she has a jacket on now. A long flowing cloak, to be precise, that seems to be the cause of all the Raven feathers and not just some dramatic affect Zarith seems to revel in. "Do you have the Moonstone?"

"Obviously," Veronica says, tossing Zarith the stone. She feels a scream wanting to escape her, the type that would leave her throat raw and probably make her lose her voice. "Now that we're here, how are you going to get Miriam?"

"Oh sweet Veronica," Zarith says with a sly smile, as she pulls a scythe from behind her back. The shaft is the 'standard' size of sixty-seven inches, and the blade is made of Onyx. It will collect whatever souls Zarith needs with ease. With a slight clanking noise as it hits the dock, Zarith leans against her scythe,

"Miriam's never left the lake." She looks away from Veronica, off into the distance. "This lake is special."

"I don't understand," Veronica says as she eyes the blade. This is starting to feel more like a trap than some potential rescue for her sister. "Are you here to get the Nixies and save Miriam, or did you bring me here to claim my soul?"

"I'm here to do a bit of both," Zarith says with a shrug, "I was told to find the Nixies who took your sister, something I've been assigned to for years. But, like I said in the café, I haven't been able to get here because of you." Zarith tilts the blade toward Veronica. "Your rage and fear has cast a spell over this lake. Nothing here has been able to be touched by Death. It's an impressive thing considering the fact you were eighteen and knew so little compared to where you are now."

"Am I being offered a job?"

"No, of course not, idiot,." Zarith walks past Veronica to the end of the dock, the blade glowing in the moonlight. A light breeze makes her cloak flow behind her as she points the blade toward the lake. "I'm here to do my job and maybe do something nice."

Veronica lets out a frustrated noise. She wants to run off the dock into the woods, away from whatever is about to happen but knows it won't help Miriam. Running won't help anything. Nor would running into the lake with some half-assed spell to make sure she won't drown. The Moonstone in her pocket doesn't seem to be playing a part in Zarith's job either and makes her feel that it was just some test to see if she would do it. "What is the Moonstone supposed to do?"

"Keep you from being seen by the Nixies. It's a bit of blind faith, to reassure you that I'm not here for you." Zarith says this in a monotone voice. "Now use it, and don't interrupt me again."

Veronica does her best to not say something snarky to Zarith and focuses on the Moonstone, on not being seen by anyone. It is a satisfying feeling to know that her reflection won't even be a thing in the damn lake she hates so very much. She hopes that this will go well, prays that whatever powers have been so kind to her for so long to have Krysten in her life, will be good to her tonight.

The lake starts to bubble like a sauna as Zarith's blade starts to glow white. The breeze picks up, the sound of thunder booms overhead, as Nixies, hundreds of them, emerge from the lake. Skin shades of blue, eyes entirely white, and hair like seaweed.

Veronica bites her lip, trying once again not to scream. Gods above, she doesn't think she will be able to stand seeing so many Nixies right now. They haunted her dreams, and now she is seeing hundreds of them face-to-face. Seeing this many is like facing a nightmare from a movie. The Nixies aren't as ugly as her mind remembers them to be. They seem translucent in the moonlight, and it disturbs her more than anything. This version of them would make her reach out for help to erase her memory of this night if she survives.

"Oh Nixies of this simple lake, your time has come," Zarith says, her voice booming like the thunder. "The Queen of Order has sent me for your souls. Do not bother fighting." Zarith starts to twirl her scythe. A slight whooshing noise almost makes Veronica laugh if it wasn't also intimidating. "Bring me Miriam, and this will be quick and easy."

"You think your precious Queen of Order can control our lives?" The Nixies speak as one, and Zarith lets out a laugh.

"I know she does," Zarith says as she swings the blade, pointing toward the center of the lake. "She is Death, and I am just a simple servant. Your time has come. Accept death gracefully."

The blade starts to glow from white to black again, "You have lived much longer than any of you have the right to," Zarith says as the Nixies' bodies start to fall one by one into the lake. Souls are pulled from the bodies into the blade of her scythe, and as the last body falls, Veronica drops the Moonstone because Miriam is in her sight. She's the same, her hairs in braids. She's in an oversized t-shirt and a one-piece bathing suit she loved that was covered in stars.

"Veronica help me. They're so mean. They keep on hurting me." Miriam's voice is as high-pitched as Veronica remembers it to be, and she's trying not to cry.

"It's going to be okay, Miriam," Zarith says, ignoring Veronica entirely. "I'm sorry it's taken so long for me to find you."

"I don't care who you are. I want my sister." Miriam says from the center of the lake, "I don't like what's happening to me. I'm scared."

"Miriam, it's going to be okay." Veronica runs now towards Zarith, not caring about the scythe and the fact it is still glowing.

Her hands are outstretched for a hug, hoping, praying that she can have this moment. "I love you. I'm so sorry. I'm so, so, sorry. You deserve better than me."

As Veronica's arms wrap around Miriam's, she feels tears streaming down her face, but she doesn't care. She's missed Miriam for so long, has hated herself for so long, and now, at least right now, she has her back in her arms. Her little sister she had failed so long ago. Was it really failure, though, when she wasn't able to control what was happening? Did that matter to the guilt she felt? No, of course not. The guilt has been eating away at her for so long. She has done so much good over the years, but this moment makes all of the guilt seem to go away.

"This part is always so annoying," Zarith mutters as Veronica and Miriam hug. "Touching, heart-to-heart moments always make this part hard." With another twirl of her Scythe, now raised above her head, she swings down and collects Miriam's soul. "I'm sorry it must be this way. I'm only doing my job."

Veronica falls to her knees, holding onto Miriam's lifeless body, now limp in her arms. This moment is something she should have expected. Something she should have prepared for, some way to counter Zarith's Scythe. And yet she hadn't. She was sloppy. This is out of her league. She should have listened to Krysten. This was a trap. She is going to die too. She can feel it in her bones as she holds onto Miriam.

"It's not your time, Veronica." Zarith says as she kneels beside Veronica and Miriam. "I won't be seeing you again for another forty years. You have many more triumphs and tragedies to experience. A relatively happy life, if I do say so myself."

"You are aware you've made an enemy of me, Zarith." Veronica says, still holding onto Miriam. It's morbid, but so is this entire event. "I will find a way to make you pay."

"You can get in line with everyone else that witnesses me doing my job, Veronica. I'm sorry this was how it had to happen, but going forward, you will no longer see me." With a snap of her pale fingers, Veronica is back in her living room, on her knees, tears streaming down her face.

"Krysten," Veronica shouts as she forces herself to stand up. Her body screams in protest, wanting nothing more than to lie down and cry. As Veronica goes to push the bedroom door open, Krysten opens it. Veronica collapses against her, tears streaming down her face once again. "You were right, and I'm sorry I didn't listen."

"I'm sorry that I wasn't there for you," Krysten says, pulling Veronica into a tight hug. "I don't know what I can do to help, but I will do whatever I can."

"Just keep on hugging me, and tomorrow, we're going to figure out how to take down a Grim Reaper."

Mimi Schweid

Mimi Schweid is a person of many talents. Writing has been her way to share her sarcastic and fantastical worlds with all that choose to listen, and others that just happen to be nearby.

She can be found at akamschweid.com and on her social media as Morganstein17.

About the Press

Eagle Heights Press, a division of Eagle Heights L.L.C., publishes thriller, fantasy, science fiction, historical fiction, paranormal romance, speculative and urban fiction, young adult, non-fiction, and more.

Find us on the web at EagleHeightsPress.com.

EagleHeightsPress

Other Titles from Eagle Heights Press

The Blood Royal Saga Vampire Series
by Delia Remington
In The Blood
Out For Blood
Trial By Blood

Soar: Indie Author Business Planner
by Delia Remington

Forthcoming Releases

Forgotten Dreams, a novella
by Melissa Shadows

Bedlam, a novella
by Karolyne Cronin

Flesh And Blood
by Delia Remington

All titles available from EagleHeightsPress.com
or online from retailers worldwide.